OUTLAWED

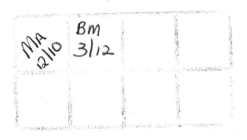

OUTLAWED

JACKSON COLE

WHEELER
CHIVERS

This Large Print edition is published by Wheeler Publishing, Waterville, Maine, USA and by BBC Audiobooks Ltd, Bath, England.
Wheeler Publishing, a part of Gale, Cengage Learning.

LIBRARY OF CONGRESS CATALOGING-IN-PUBLICATION DATA

Cole, Jackson.
    Outlawed / by Jackson Cole. — Large print ed.
      p. cm. — (Wheeler Publishing large print western)
    Originally published: Bath : Gunsmoke, 1954.
    ISBN-13: 978-1-59722-973-9 (pbk. : alk. paper)
    ISBN-10: 1-59722-973-3 (pbk. : alk. paper)
    1. Texas Rangers—Fiction. 2. Texas—Fiction. 3. Large type
books. I. Title.
PS3505.O2685O96 2009
813'.52—dc22   2009002068

BRITISH LIBRARY CATALOGUING-IN-PUBLICATION DATA AVAILABLE

Published in 2009 in the U.S. by arrangement with Golden West Literary Agency.
Published in 2009 in the U.K. by arrangement with Golden West Literary Agency.

U.K. Hardcover: 978 1 408 44186 2 (Chivers Large Print)
U.K. Softcover: 978 1 408 44187 9 (Camden Large Print)

Printed in the United States of America
1 2 3 4 5 6 7 13 12 11 10 09

OUTLAWED

1.

Standing at the bar in the border town of Sanders, Jim Hatfield had plenty to occupy his mind. The tall, broad-shouldered Texas Ranger with the black hair, hawk face, and long, black-lashed eyes of a curious shade of green, chuckled as he thought of the bad temper Captain Bill McDowell had been in when he left the Ranger Post the day before.

"Dang it! I don't know what to make of it!" McDowell had said, hammering his desk with a gnarled fist. "First time I ever knew the Border Tribes to get together on anything, but unless everything I hear is a danged lie, they've done it now. Apaches, Comanches, Lipans, Yaquis, and all the rest. Rumors of a general uprising flying in every direction. And if they are all banded together and all cut loose at once, as the reports I get lead me to believe, this section of Texas will be plain hell. I'd have never given Pedro Cartina credit for having the brains to pull a thing like this."

"Are you sure it's really Cartina who's back of it?" Hatfield had asked.

"Who else?" Captain Bill had shot back at him. "Cartina is the best-known bandit leader and arms-smuggler along the Border. Poses as a liberator who will free the common people of Mexico from oppression. And he's got plenty of deluded fools believing in him. We know he's nothing but a snake-blooded robber and killer, but south of the Rio Grande too many people think otherwise. And he has a way with the tribes; he's proven that before. What his influence over them is I'll never know, but when he talks the chiefs listen."

"I've learned considerable about Cartina," Hatfield had said thoughtfully. "For the life of me I can't see him as a man capable of carrying out such a scheme. Not without help from some more able man. It's just too big for Cartina."

"Who else?" Captain Bill had repeated. "Unless old Tom Weston has a loco notion about leading a raid into Mexico and over-turning the Diaz government. There's quite a few folks believe in *him*. But even if he did try a crazy stunt like William Walker did years ago, the Border Indians on the rampage would be the last thing he'd want. If

8

there was anything to prove they are being incorporated into an invading force, that would be different, but nothing like that has come to light. No, Cartina is the man back of it all, but I'll admit I wouldn't have given him credit for having so much sense.

"And there's another angle that causes me to suspect Cartina more than anybody else. All the outlaw bands south of the Rio Grande are getting together too. Used to be they were as badly split up as the tribes and hated each other's guts. But of late they've been working in unison. I can see Cartina's hand in that, and it's bad. We've been up against some tough problems, Jim, but never anything like this."

"Looks like you might be right," Hatfield had had to admit. "But just the same, when I ride over to Sanders tomorrow, I'm going to have a talk with Tom Weston."

"Not a bad notion," Captain Bill had agreed. "He's crazy as a coot, but he might know something. You think you might get a line on Cartina over there?"

"With luck, I may nab *him!*"

"Go to it! This thing is getting out of hand, and if it busts loose it'll give Anton Page a double-barrel of ammunition to use in his campaign against the Rangers. I can just see the headlines of his newspapers now: ANOTHER EXAMPLE OF RANGER INEFFICIENCY. ALERT LAW ENFORCEMENT COULD HAVE PREVENTED THIS TRAGEDY. BUT DO THE RANGERS WANT LAW ENFORCEMENT? THAT'S WHAT THE PEOPLE OF TEXAS WANT TO KNOW. That'll sound nice, won't it, with the headway he's already made."

"By the way," Hatfield had said, "I hear Page has been visiting Tom Weston of late."

"Probably trying to enlist his support against the Rangers, eh?" Captain Bill had snorted. "That would be a fine kettle of fish, if Weston threw in with him. Weston's got a big following all over the state. People take his word for things. I don't know whether Page could talk him into it, but he'll try anything."

Hatfield didn't underestimate Anton Page. In fact, as he sipped his drink in the Sanders's saloon, he stopped thinking about yesterday's conversation with McDowell and concentrated on Anton Page.

The story was that Page got his start running "wet cows" across the Rio Grande and smuggling goods into Mexico. True or not, Page was now a man of wealth and influence. He owned a string of newspapers, among other things, and he knew how to use them for personal gain. For some time, he had been waging a campaign of vilification, innuendo and half-truths against the Texas Rangers. Hatfield knew that Page had his eye on the governor's seat and the fabulously rich state lands of Texas and schemed to get both, and if he wasn't stopped, he might very well succeed. That was the reason for his vicious campaign against the Rangers. Page saw the famous corps of peace officers as the one obstacle in his quest for power. He planned to eliminate the Rangers, or at least discredit them.

Some of the older Ranger captains were inclined to scoff at Page and his attempt, but Jim Hatfield and Captain Bill McDowell took Page very seriously. Any really big trouble along the Border would play right into Page's hands. He was probably laughing up his sleeve right now, Hatfield thought, as he sat back and watched events shaping up to his advantage, without him having to lift a hand himself.

No, Jim Hatfield did not underestimate Anton Page as a threat to the Rangers. Such things had been done before, and could be again. But he did underestimate the man's cunning.

As he stood at the bar, Hatfield was under

discussion. Two lean, hard-faced men occupying a table in a shadowy corner of the room never took their eyes off his broad back.

"It's Hatfield, all right," one said in low tones. "I saw him once, and he's the sort you never forget. Yes, that's our man, all right."

"Uh-huh," the other returned, with scant enthusiasm, "We've found him, but now what the hell we going to do with him?"

"You know the General's orders," said the first speaker. "We've got to do it. But for God's sake, watch your step and don't slip. He's poison. You know his reputation. The fastest and deadliest man with a gun in the whole Southwest. And that hellion's fists are as bad as his bullet. If he hits you the next thing you know is when the doctor says, 'Sit up and take this!' We've got to go through with it, but we've got to be careful."

"The General seems awful anxious to get hold of him, all right."

"And why not? He's the key man. If we can bring Hatfield around to our way of thinking, he'll swing the rest of the Rangers into line. Even Bill McDowell will follow Hatfield's lead. McDowell sets a heap of store by him. It was McDowell who got him into the Rangers. A funny story, too."

"How's that?"

"Well, it happened quite a few years ago, when Hatfield was a young feller, just out of college. He studied engineering, I understand and would likely have made a name for himself at it. He's used his knowledge more than once in Ranger work. It seemed some widelooping buzzards shot his dad in the course of running off his big trail herd. Understand the old man never had a chance. It was a snake-blooded killing. Young Jim was all set to run down those sidewinders and do for them. But before he set out, McDowell got hold of him and showed him that riding the vengeance trail on your own is mighty bad business and likely to end you up on the wrong side of the law. He made Hatfield a proposition. Told him he'd take him on with the Rangers and that running down his dad's killers would be his first chore. Well, Hatfield ran the buzzards down, all right, and did for them, one after another. Took quite a while, though, and I reckon he got to like Ranger work. Anyhow, he stayed with the outfit. Worked alone to run down his dad's killers, and most always worked alone since. That's how he came by the name, Lone Wolf. Now, just say 'Lone Wolf' and an outlaw bunch

13

gets the shivers. He's the best-known and most highly respected Ranger of them all. If we can get Hatfield to come in with us, we'll get the whole Ranger outfit without much trouble. The General knows what he's doing."

"And it's up to us to bring him in," the other observed gloomily. "Lord! what a chore! Well, let's get out of here and get set. I hope to God nothing slips."

"It had better not or we'll be talking it over with St. Peter before morning!"

Engrossed in his own thoughts and his plan to contact old Tom Weston, Hatfield did not notice the departure of the pair. After he finished his drink, he decided to go to bed.

Still heavy with thought, he left the saloon, turned into a side street and made his way toward the small livery stable in which he had quartered his horse. Wanting to be within reach of his big sorrel, Goldy, he had obtained a room over the stalls, a room which was reached by climbing a stair hung against the outer wall of the building.

As he turned into the dimly lighted passage that led to the room, he looked squarely into the muzzles of two guns. Behind the guns stood two men, eyes glinting in the shadow of low-drawn hatbrims.

14

"Take it easy, feller," said a quiet voice. "Reaching for your irons would sure be fatal."

Hatfield did not move, nor did he answer. There was something in the quiet tones of the man who spoke that precluded argument. He instantly sized up the men with whom he was dealing.

"All right," continued the man in the shadow, "turn around, slow, hands away from your belt."

Hatfield obeyed. Instantly a gun muzzle was jammed against his ribs. Expert hands unbuckled his cartridge belts and whisked them away, felt at his pockets for a possible knife, probed under his arms for shoulder holsters and ran exploring fingers along the tops of his boots.

"Don't miss a bet," Hatfield mused. "These gents know their business."

The man who had searched him stepped back. The gun muzzle was removed from his ribs.

"Down the stairs, turn to the right and keep moving till you're told to stop," said a voice.

Hatfield obeyed, passing around the corner of the stable and into an open space dimly lit by stars that seemed to brush the mountain tops with silver fingers. He was

15

halted near the blank wall of a mine building. A low word from his captors and a third man appeared, leading four horses.

"Ride the roan," said the man who had done all the talking.

As soon as he mounted, Hatfield's ankles were swiftly and securely lashed to the stirrup straps. The three men mounted and the little cavalcade moved out of town by way of dimly lit and almost deserted side streets. A few minutes later they turned into a trail that wound through the hills to the northeast. For nearly an hour the craggy slopes shouldered against the track, then they began to fall away and the trail dipped toward rangeland rolling and tossing under the stars.

Hatfield was not particularly alarmed for his personal safety. If his captors had intended him bodily harm, they would have translated their purpose into action long before. His chief emotion was one of curiosity.

In the course of the ride he refrained from making comment or asking questions. He knew that either would be a waste of breath. These men were undoubtedly acting under orders, and they were not the sort to discuss them. During the hour they were practically speechless themselves. An occasional profane comment on the roughness of the road and a remark or two about incidents in town were the extent of the conversation.

But if Hatfield's vocal cords were idle, his keen mind was not. Plan after plan for escape was formulated only to be discarded. His bound ankles and the alertness of his captors made any attempt little short of suicide. Also, his curiosity as to what was back of all this was paramount. There must be some urgent motive back of the attack on him. He felt pretty sure the men knew who he was. Kidnaping a Texas Ranger was no light matter; it was likely to be fraught with unpleasant repercussions for the perpetrators of the outrage. Captain McDowell and others knew he was in Sanders and if he turned up missing for any length of time, all holy hell would be raised. Oh, well, he had been in tough spots before and had always managed to extricate himself. So why bother? He philosophically resigned himself to present conditions and was content to let developments shape his future actions. Meanwhile, holding himself ready to take advantage of any opportunity that might present itself, he proceeded to enjoy the beauty of the night.

It was early autumn and although the days were still hot, there was enough crispness in the night air to quicken the blood. Overhead the bonfire stars of Texas glowed like grapes of light, and as the night grew older a great white moon soared up from behind the eastern peaks and flooded the rolling prairie with molten silver. It shone on grove and thicket and lonely crag, making of each a jet mystery edged with pale flame. In the mellow light, the black bulk of a big and rambling ranchhouse stood out in sharp detail, as did barns and bunkhouse and other buildings. The winding gravel drive that led to the ranchhouse veranda was pale bronze etched in dull copper.

At the steps of the veranda the company halted. Hatfield's feet were released and he was dismounted and marched up the steps. A door opened and he entered a large room, blinking at the light. When his vision cleared he saw a table in front of a cheerfully blazing fire of logs in a wide fireplace.

On the far side of the table sat a big old man with a magnificent mane of crinkly white hair sweeping back from his dome-shaped forehead, a high-featured craggy face running to a great eagle-beak of a nose, a firm though humorous mouth, and frosty blue eyes burning with a strange brilliance. The eyes were fixed on the Texas Ranger and he nodded in a friendly fashion.

"Sit down, Lieutenant Hatfield," he invited cordially, gesturing to a chair on the opposite side of the table.

Hatfield was instantly struck by the use of the military title, for, although it merely designated his rank in the Ranger corps, the old man spoke it as an article of war. But he merely nodded acknowledgment and sat down.

"Thanks, General," he said.

Old Tom Weston picked up the heavy guns that Hatfield's captors laid on the table beside him. He examined the big Colts with the air of a connoisseur, laid them down and turned his burning eyes on Hatfield.

"Fine weapons, Lieutenant," he complimented, "the tools of a master workman, too fine to be used against your countrymen."

Hatfield said nothing. He preferred to leave the burden of explanation to Weston. The old statesman, skilled in debate, would instantly seize on any remark he might make and turn it against him, and he did not care to give Weston any more advantage than his natural ability conferred upon him. This characteristic of Hatfield's had once caused Captain Bill McDowell to say that Hatfield had something of that gift which General Grant so often used to confound his enemies and even, at times, bewilder his friends — an amazing gift for saying nothing.

"Yes," repeated Weston, "too fine to be used against your fellow-countrymen, your natural friends, those on whose side you should always fight."

Jim Hatfield spoke, his level glance meeting the other's burning gaze unflinchingly, "I am fighting in their cause, General Weston, and have been for quite a few years now, and I propose to continue fighting in their cause. And now, General, don't you think a bit of explanation is in order? This is a rather high-handed proceeding — grabbing a Texas Ranger at gun point and bringing him here in bonds. A waste of risk and energy, too. I had planned to visit you soon, on my own accord."

"There was no other way," Weston replied sententiously. "Had you come to this house willingly, the laws of hospitality would have forbade your being detained, or threatened. I have something to tell you. Please listen, attentively. If any remark should occur to you while I am speaking, you can reserve it for some more opportune time."

For a moment Weston paused, gazing at the march of the shadows on the wall. Then he began to talk. Hatfield listened at first with mild interest, then in startled amazement as Weston outlined, in detail, his Grand Plan.

Old Tom Weston dreamed a great dream. It was not new with Weston, this dream of conquest and empire. A man greater than he had once dreamed of joining Texas, Mexico, Arizona, New Mexico and part of California in one strong and prosperous federation that would stand shoulder to shoulder with America, but on independent feet: Sam Houston, commander in chief of the Texan army that defeated Santa Anna at San Jacinto and secured Texan independence, first President of the new republic, United States Senator, Governor of the state had evolved that "Grand Plan," as he called it. Tom Weston, when little more than a boy, had marched under the banner of the great Captain and was one of his most trusted scouts. Weston had heard the Grand Plan from Sam Houston's own lips and his ambitions had been fired by it.

But the Civil War had intervened and Sam Houston, loyal to the Union, had died an impoverished and embittered man and the Grand Plan had vanished into the dust of the grave.

Tom Weston had gone on to fame and glory. A two-star general in the Confederate

Army, of whom General Grant himself, had said, "Had he, instead of Hood, been given supreme command at Atlanta, General Sherman's historic march might have been another story." Pioneer, statesman, cattle rancher of untold wealth, now that he was old, he was a power in the land. His following was large, especially among the older Texans of the Border country, his influence strong all over the state. And Tom Weston had always felt that it was for him to catch the torch that fell from the failing hand of Sam Houston. He had never favored annexation. He believed that had it never happened, Texas would have been spared the anguish of the Civil War and the trouble and turmoil that followed.

And now Weston felt the time was ripe for action. Mexico writhed in the iron grip of a dictator and longed for freedom. Texas was in the throes of a strong agrarian movement that was causing much unrest. New Mexico and Arizona were plagued by turbulent outlaw bands and trouble along the Border.

Seated in his spacious ranchhouse, the grim and wonderfully wise old man watched the great fire dance on his wide hearth and the fantastic shadows keep perfect time on wall and ceiling. Not less fantastic than the play of the shadows was the dream of the old soldier and statesman. He saw a long column of men at whose head rode the man who had proved at Monterey, at Buena Vista, at Atlanta what he and his stern Texans could do. Good Mexican guides would lead the advance. A thousand swarthy Indians — Kickapoos, Creeks, Cherokees, Kiowas, and Comanches — would scout, trail and sky. And the core of his "Army of Liberation" would be the famed Texas Rangers.

He, the old general, would carry American civilization and progress southward. For Mexico would come peace and prosperity and advancement, and the bands of empire would be firmly riveted. Yes, to him the torch had been thrown; it was for him to hold it high.

Weston had ceased speaking and sat brooding into the fire. He seemed to have forgotten the presence of his listener.

Hatfield also sat silent, evaluating what he had heard. It was bizarre, fantastic, but unless Weston's insane ambitions were curbed, they might well drench the Border country in blood.

Hatfield did not impugn Tom Weston's motives. He knew the old statesman and patriot was sincere in his beliefs. But Weston was still living in the days of long ago, the days of the Texas Republic, when such things might have been possible. Time had marched on, but Tom Weston had been standing at the side of the trail, heedless of the long procession of events and developments that made his vision utterly impracticable. Weston could not see that what he advocated could only end in suffering and tragedy. Hatfield, with the more penetrating vision of youth, saw it all too clearly. He saw, too, that Weston's mistaken ambitions would provide opportunity for such men as Pedro Cartina and Anton Page, the one a ruthless outlaw, the other a wily politician and opportunist. And Hatfield understood now the reason why he had been brought a prisoner to the Running W ranchhouse. Weston hoped to assimilate the Rangers into his "Army of Liberation," to make of the outfit the hard core of his forces, and relied on Hatfield's influence and prestige to help him attain that end. What came next corroborated his shrewd deduction.

Tom Weston raised his big head, turned and gazed expectantly at the Ranger.

"Now that you have heard," he said, "will you join us? We can rely on your assistance?"

Jim Hatfield smiled, a trifle sadly, and slowly shook his head.

"No, General," he said, his voice free from

emotion, "no, I won't join you. I grant you think you're right and doing the right thing, but I'm telling you once and for all, you're wrong! The thing you propose to do can't mean anything but needless killing and suffering and trouble. It won't work, General, it won't get you anywhere." Raising his hand to halt the other's interruption, he continued:

"You're living in the past. Once, when old General Sam Houston first thought this thing out, it might have worked, but not now. It means attacking a friendly country that's having trouble enough of its own right now, and fighting against your own country as well. The folks of our country won't back you up any more than the folks down below the Line will. It will mean, before it is finished, Federal intervention and something corresponding to the horrible years of the Reconstruction period.

"You won't be serving Texas, General, and you won't be serving the men who think anything you do is bound to be right and will follow you regardless. You're playing into the hands of buzzards like Pedro Cartina, who are always sitting on a limb, waiting for someone to get hurt so they can take over and pick the bones. You will be providing such men as Anton Page opportunity to forward their own selfish and ruthless schemes."

Before Weston could reply, Hatfield leaned far across the table and the intensity and force in his bronzed face beat down for the moment the fire rising in Weston's blue eyes. His words drove at the old warrior like bullets.

"Forget it, General," he urged. "You join with *me* and help clean up the Border country and destroy the schemes of Anton Page, who is out to destroy the Rangers, the only force he fears, for his own avaricious and despicable ends. With your help there's nothing to it. Lighten your grip on the capital and let them turn the Texas Rangers loose on the job of running down Page and Cartina. Yes, I know it's your influence that's got the outfit roped. Ease up on the rope, General and let the boys take over. You've always been the biggest man this section ever produced. Stay the biggest, General. Don't let your ambition be the tool of Page and Cartina and *their* ambitions."

For a moment it seemed that Hatfield's utter and selfless sincerity might triumph; but as the firelight flickered and the shadows climbed along the wall, the old leader again saw his mighty dream marching amid the shadow of the future. The indecision left his face and the strange fire again burned in his eyes.

And seeing that wild light rise and grow, Hatfield realized that the man who sat opposite him was mad — mad with his dreams of power and conquest made of his visions based on the facts of yesterday but with no place upon which to stand today. From the wild blue eyes sanity had fled.

Weston spoke, in an almost inaudible mutter, as if communing with his own thoughts, justifying himself to himself, beating down facts with the bludgeon of self-deception —

"Cartina is a patriot, and Anton Page is my friend."

Hatfield leaned forward again. "Cartina is not a patriot; he is just a snake-blooded bandit working for himself and nobdy else. And Anton Page is a friend only to — Anton Page." Again the undeniable ring of sincerity, the simple statement of a truth.

Tom Weston gazed across the table and as he measured the six feet and more of Jim Hatfield, there was in his gaze the admiration of one fighting man for another; but as he fingered the long-barreled guns his face hardened.

"This is war, Lieutenant Hatfield," he said, "a war in which your country — your people — are engaged. If you align yourself against your country and your people, you are not only an enemy, you are a traitor, and yours will be a traitor's fate. I give you until tomorrow morning to think it over and decide. Join us and your place will be second only to mine — yours will be power and glory and the admiration and respect of your countrymen. Refuse — the firing squad and a traitor's unmarked grave!"

He gestured to the silent men standing behind the Ranger's chair.

"All right, Hatfield," said one, "let's go."

They led him across the big room, down a long corridor, unlocked a massive door and swung it back, revealing a much smaller room lighted by a single lamp. It contained a chair, a bed and a table. The one window was barred with iron. In the far wall was a second door as massive as the first, also doubtless securely locked.

The heavy door closed behind Hatfield. He heard the bolt shoot home.

Jim Hatfield knew it was well past midnight. Judging from the way events were shaping, unless he could do something about it, he figured that he had some six or seven hours to live.

2.

Hatfield sat down on the bed and rolled a cigarette. He needed a little time to ponder what he had learned. The thing was staggering in its magnitude and possibilities. And it shed a new and unexpected light on the recent happenings along the Border. Hatfield had been inclined to string along with Captain McDowell's contention that Pedro Cartina was master-minding the Border trouble. Now he wasn't so sure. The insane old dreamer might have conceived that a general uprising of Border tribes, in cahoots with the outlaw bands, might work to his advantage. It would undoubtedly provide a diversion — a diversion that would keep every peace officer in southwest Texas occupied and might well expedite Weston's contemplated sudden drive into Mexico. It was hard to think of Weston being so callous. Hatfield had to remind himself that this was not the Tom Weston of former days. Obsessed with an idea, he might feel that the end justified any means he saw fit to employ.

Impressed on Hatfield was the urgent necessity to escape from his prison before morning. Not only did his own life hang in the balance; more important, to his way of thinking, the very existence of the Rangers as a free and independent law enforcement agency might well be at stake. He alone, aside from Weston's most trusted followers, knew exactly what the General had in mind. He could put that knowledge to good use, if he could just get the chance to use it.

"We'll wait till things quiet down a little and then we'll see what can be done," he decided.

Relaxing on the narrow bed, he pondered the complex character of Tom Weston. A rabid Secessionist, he had not believed in slavery and had owned no slaves. An officer in the Confederate Army, he had been a staunch admirer of Abraham Lincoln, with whom he had enjoyed a warm friendship. A man with the common touch and the ambitions of a king. And now in the winter of his life he was embarked on a mad enterprise that could only end in disaster.

It was not the futility of Tom Weston's ambitions that concerned Hatfield. It was the inevitable sorrow and suffering that would follow in the wake of his mistaken endeavors. This Hatfield had resolved to prevent at all cost; but at the moment, he reflected grimly, there was a mighty good chance that somebody else would have to handle the chore. He got up and gave the room a careful once-over.

The log walls were thick, the window bars stout and deeply imbedded in the heavy framework and the stone sill. He took hold of one and put forth all his great strength. The bar quivered a little, no more. He tried it a few more times with no better results. There was nothing in the room that could serve as a pry. He examined the door in the far wall. It was locked, all right, and the big key appeared to be in the outside of the lock.

The door by which he had entered the room opened inward. It was secured in place by heavy iron hinges. He examined the hinge screws, fumbled at a cunningly concealed secret pocket in his broad leather belt and drew forth his Ranger badge, the famous silver star set on a silver circle. Once before he had escaped from a locked room by removing the hinge screws, employing the steel-backed badge as a screwdriver. He set the edge into one of the screw heads and put forth a torsion pressure.

But it didn't work this time. The big screws were driven deep in the seasoned oak timber. He only succeeded in bending the curved rim of the badge. After several futile attempts he gave it up. He walked back to the window and looked out. The window opened onto a side yard of the ranchhouse. In the near distance loomed the dark bulk of a barn, etched in the silver of the moon. He returned to the bed and sat down.

Jim Hatfield was not one to give in to despair, but he was forced to admit a deepening depression.

" 'Pears anybody put in here is here to stay," he mused. "Chances are there's a fellow in the next room with a gun handy listening for any untoward noise in here. Beginning to look like curtains."

Despite his pompous and grandiloquent phraseology, old Tom Weston had meant just what he said, and his fanatical followers would carry out his orders without hesitation or compunction.

Gradually the normal sounds of living in the big ranchhouse ebbed and muffled, and finally stilled completely. Hatfield lay motionless on the bunk, thinking, planning. His final resolve was, when they came for him he would make a desperate attempt to down his captors and perhaps obtain a gun with which he might shoot his way to freedom. If not more than two men came to lead him from his prison he might have a chance, although cold reason told him that in any event it would be infinitesimally small. Better to die fighting than to stand blindfolded before the raised rifles, waiting for the sharp bark of command that would tighten fingers on the triggers. Decided on just what he would do, he relaxed, rolled a cigarette and proceeded to enjoy his smoke. The great establishment was deathly still now. No slightest sound blunted the sharp edge of the silence. Apparently men and beasts were all asleep.

Suddenly he was conscious of a sound, a light, persistent tapping that seemed to come from the direction of the barred window. He swung his feet to the floor and silently crossed the room. Etched in the moonlight outside the window, he saw a face, a piquante little face framed in curly hair that smoldered like reddish flame, a face that at first seemed all great apprehensive blue eyes.

"Hush!" she whispered, laying a sun-golden finger on her vividly red lips. "Hush! Do just as I say. Here is a key to the back door. Unlock it and come out. Bring the key with you. And oh, be quiet!"

Hatfield did not stop to ask questions or wonder about this most unexpected deliverance. He took the key she extended to him and did just what she said. The key turned silently in the lock. The door swung back with equal silence. Hatfield stepped out, closing the door behind him.

"Lock it and give me the key," came a whisper from the shadows alongside the wall.

Hatfield obeyed. He turned, the key in his hand as she stepped from the shadows.

She was tiny, her bright head not even coming to his shoulder, slender, graceful. The close-fitting robe she wore showed alluring curves and the luscious upper swell of her ripe young breasts.

"Hush!" she repeated. "You are still in great danger. My uncle is mad! mad! He has been that way for a long time. Of late he has been steadily worse. I heard everything tonight. He meant it when he said you would be shot this morning if you didn't consent to join with him in his crazy enterprise. Here are your guns. I took them from the table as he slept in his chair. He often does that lately."

Hatfield buckled on the big Colts and felt a hundred per cent better. He spoke for the first time.

"But won't you get into trouble if he learns you turned me loose?" he protested.

Her firm little chin went up proudly. "If you can take the risks you do for the sake of others, I guess I can afford to take a much smaller one," she said. "My uncle believes

34

in what he is doing; a more honest man never lived. But he is old, and his followers are old. They are living in the past. It is men like yourself who have the true vision, who see things as they are. I am only too glad to be able to help a little in your fight to prevent bloodshed and suffering."

Hatfield's interest quickened at this evidence of depth of character and understanding.

"A girl to ride the river with!" he chuckled.

She dimpled at him as he paid her the greatest compliment the rangeland has to offer.

"Very likely he won't suspect me," she added. "Of late he is suspicious of nearly everyone, even of those he should trust the most. It is part of his madness. And even if he does, I don't think he will be too hard on me. He adored my mother, his dead sister — I think she was the only thing he ever really loved — and folks say I am greatly like her, although she was a great beauty in her day. When my hair is dressed as it is now, as she used to wear hers, he can never resist me."

Looking at her, Hatfield thought it unlikely that any man could.

"You must slip across to the barn," she continued. "Take the horse in the first stall

— he's very gentle. His saddle and bridle are hanging just inside the door. The moon will give enough light for you to see. Then lead him around the barn and through the grove to the trail. There is a guard stationed where the drive joins the trail. There always is, day and night. I don't know what you will do about him. He can see along the trail for a long ways."

"How about cutting across the prairie?" Hatfield asked.

"That won't do either," she said. "There are more guards at the edge of the grove around the ranchhouse. And you can make better going on the trail, if you can only reach it."

"I'll reach it," Hatfield promised grimly. "Ma'am, there isn't any use trying to thank you for what you did — words are rather inadequate when a life is at stake — but I do appreciate it. Mind telling me your name?"

"Sylvia," she said. "Sylvia Mayfield. I know yours — it's Mr. Hatfield. I heard it mentioned."

"I prefer Jim where my friends are concerned, especially those to whom I am greatly indebted," he said.

She smiled, a dimple showing at one corner of her red mouth. "All right — Jim," she answered. "I must slip back to my room now. I hope you make it all right."

"I will, thanks to you," he said. "Good-bye, Sylvia. Or rather, *hasta luego!*"

" 'Till we meet again!' " she translated softly. "*Vaya usted con Dios!* Go you with God!"

She melted back into the shadows. Hatfield's keen ears caught the light whisper of her steps fading away around the building. He glanced about and then, hands close to the butts of his guns, stole across the open space to the barn. He found the door unlocked. Swinging it back gently he could see the dim outlines of the stalls. He sidled into the first one. Its occupant blew softly through his nose as Hatfield stroked his glossy neck. Groping about, the Ranger found saddle and bridle hanging from a peg. To slip off the halter, replace it with bridle and bit, cinch the saddle into place was the work of a moment. He led the docile animal from the barn, closed the door and made his way through the grove the girl had indicated. The horse's hoofs made practically no sound on the soft earth.

Walking slowly, Hatfield reached the fringe of the belt of growth and the moon-splashed trail lay before him. And standing back in the shadow a little ways, he made out the figure of the guard, rifle cradled in his arm.

Hatfield debated his next move. He had no desire to kill or seriously injure the man. He had no feeling of enmity toward the misguided believers in the old zealot. But he had to get past him. The trail stretched straight for nearly a mile and in the bright moonlight a rider would be a settin' quail for a good rifleman. Finally he left the horse standing with the split reins trailing on the ground, confident that the well-trained animal would not move. He stole along in the shadow toward the unsuspecting guard. Everything went nicely until he was almost within arm's length of the man. Then the unexpected happened. His foot came down on a dry stick hidden under the thin carpet of fallen leaves. It broke with a sharp crack. The guard jumped, whirled around, the rifle coming to his shoulder. Hatfield lunged for the barrel, caught it and forced it up as the other pulled trigger. The explosion was like a thunderclap in the still night. The bullet whined skyward. Hatfield wrenched the rifle from the other and cast it aside. Then the man was upon him. Confident in his own great strength, Hatfield met him breast to breast. The steely fingers of his right hand clamped on the guard's throat. His other hand gripped his wrist.

But the fellow was no weakling. He writhed, jerked, butted, beat at Hatfield with his free hand. The Ranger hugged his face against his breast and tightened his throttling grip. In the distance he could hear the shouts of aroused men. The door of the bunkhouse banged open. Questions were yelled. Hatfield put forth every atom of his strength. The other's struggles grew feeble. Another instant and he went limp. Hatfield dropped the unconscious man to the ground and raced back to where he had left the horse, praying that the cayuse had not become alarmed by the racket and bolted. With a deep breath of relief he found it standing at the edge of the growth, snorting, rolling its eyes and trembling. He swung into the saddle and sent the animal charging out onto the trail. Behind sounded the pad of running feet, then a crackle of gunfire. He thankfully recognized the sharper explosions of six-guns. Unless somebody had thought to bring a rifle and was even now taking careful aim, he had a chance. He instinctively stiffened for the tearing impact of a bullet, winced a moment later as a deeper boom told that somebody had at last fetched a long gun. But now he was far down the trail. He heard the slug whine past. Another followed it, closer. A third was well to one side.

"Guess we made it," he muttered, bending low in the saddle and urging his mount to greater speed. Behind sounded the distant thud of pursuing hoofs.

The horse, recognizing a master hand, gave its best. Hatfield quickly realized that Sylvia Mayfield knew what she was about when she told him to take the animal in the first stall. It was very likely old Tom's pet saddle horse.

"You aren't quite Goldy," he remarked, patting the horse's neck, "but you come about as close as any *caballo* I've forked in quite a while."

As he rode, Hatfield pondered his next move. As he saw it, he had two courses of action open. He could forget the whole episode or he could get a troop together, ride up to the ranchhouse and arrest Tom Weston and his followers. The latter, however, would mean trouble and would very probably result in bloodshed, which he was anxious to avoid. Moreover, he was highly doubtful if he would be able to make a case against Weston stick. It would be his unsupported word against the general's, and if Weston chose to deny the incident, with sentiment what it was in the section, the whole matter would very likely be tossed out of court. Nothing would be gained and it would be another talking point for those who, with Anton Page at their head, maintained that the Rangers were not only outmoded, but actually hand-in-glove with the outlaw element. Preposterous as the contention was, Hatfield knew that it posed a real threat to the existence of the law enforcement body. Page's newspapers were hammering on the theme and Page's henchmen were spreading the slanders by word of mouth.

Captain McDowell and other Ranger captains were inclined to scoff at Page's efforts: but Hatfield felt differently. There was precedent. The Rangers actually had been dissolved once before, to all practical purposes, by a carpetbagger governor, and the notorious State Police substituted until an aroused populace had forced the capital to disband the Police and re-organize the Rangers. And now Anton Page was using much the same tactics the press of the state had used against the State Police, the difference being that the allegations against the Police were supported by the facts. In the present case of the Rangers it was a campaign of innuendo. One of the most serious charges, the hardest to combat, was Page's contention that the Rangers continually invoked *la ley de fuga,* literally translated, the "law of escape," to put away prisoners whose testimony might be detrimental to the body. Headlines of Page's papers screamed:

KILLED IN ATTEMPTING TO ESCAPE!
KILLED WHILE RESISTING ARREST!

"These are two expressions," wrote a Page editor, *"that are fast coming to have a melancholy and terrible significance to the people of western Texas. They furnish the brief epitaph to the scores who have fallen and are falling victims to the ignorance, the arrogance, or the brutality of those charged with the execution of the law."*

And —

"By the abolition of this outmoded and corrupt body, the people will be delivered from as infernal an engine of oppression as has ever crushed a people beneath the heel of God's sunlight. As a class these miscreants posing as law enforcement officers are the most wolfish-looking set of men that have ever been employed on any public duty in this country."

There was plenty more in the same vein.

And to move against Weston, Hatfield

reasoned, would be to give Page more material to work on and elicit louder screams of persecution and Ranger tyranny. It would be best, he decided, to forget the whole business.

He did not anticipate any retaliatory action on the part of Weston. He was convinced the old fighter had enough sporting blood in his veins to chuckle over the mischance, once his initial anger had cooled. And he, Hatfield, would not suffer in Weston's esteem by his unexpected coup. Moreover, his escape would have a disquieting effect on Weston and his men. Their opinion of the Texas Rangers despite Page, was high, and his exploit would not tend to lower that opinion. The story was bound to get out and it would not strengthen Weston's position in the Border country, nor at Austin, the capital. Well satisfied with the outcome of the night's adventure, he dismissed the incident and turned his mind to more pressing matters.

The stars were paling from gold to silver and the eastern sky flushing a delicate rose when Hatfield dismounted, turned the big horse's head and with a friendly slap sent him cantering back up the trail. He knew the intelligent animal would have no trouble finding its way back to the ranch.

"And quite likely you'll meet some sleepy and bad-tempered gents on the way, anyhow," he chuckled. "They'll keep you company home."

Ahead, twinkled the lights of Sanders. Hatfield made his way to the cattle and mining town, which was still valiantly celebrating payday, and reached the livery stable. After first assuring himself that Goldy, his big sorrel, was all right, he slipped up the stairs to his room, carefully bolted the door behind him and went to bed, taking care to assure himself that the single window could not be attacked from the outside. He did not anticipate further trouble, but he was taking no chances. He would not be caught a second time.

3.

Hatfield slept until noon and awoke ravenously hungry. A little restaurant around the corner took care of that. He was enjoying a leisurely smoke after eating when a slender, dark-faced man in rangeland clothes entered and glanced expectantly about. Hatfield knew him to be a Kiowa scout attached to Ranger Post headquarters at Franklin. He bad been hoping the man would show up today. It was the second reason for Hatfield's being in Sanders.

"Well?" he asked as the Kiowa approached the table.

"Cartina meets with Kepnau's Comanches," the Kiowa replied laconically.

"Where?"

"I learned no more," said the Kiowa, who apparently did not believe in wasting words. "In Kepnau's village in the Chisos country, doubtless. You know where that?"

"Approximately," Hatfield replied.

"Indians talk the smoke talk today, you see and tell," said the Kiowa.

"I can't read the stuff, but I may be able to get an idea as to the location and the route used from it," Hatfield replied. "Okay, Felipe, you did a good chore. Get back on the job and try and learn something else."

"You take troop with you?" asked Felipe.

"No time to go to the Post and back," Hatfield demurred. "Be lucky to make it down there from here in time."

"Dangerous. Cartina bad."

"Can't be helped," Hatfield replied. "Have to take the chance."

"Good hunting!"

The taciturn Kiowa stalked out. Hatfield chuckled, pinched out the butt of his cigarette and went to get his horse.

"If things work out right, we may rid the

Border country of a major pest," he told the sorrel as he headed south by west toward where the Chisos Mountains, strange, mani-colored, reared their mighty bulk against the sky. All afternoon he rode, with the fantastic peaks looming taller and more ominous and the surrounding country growing wilder and more desolate. Finally, atop a tall ridge with an overhang of cliff throwing its crest in the shadow, he pulled up, hooked one long leg comfortably over the saddle horn and rolled a cigarette.

From where he sat, the country was spread out below him like a map. The evening was singularly clear and bright with no wind. The low-lying sun sent rays of level light that gold-tinged the lucid air. Every detail of the landscape was sharply defined.

"Perfect for them," he mused. "Signals can be seen for miles. Well, hope Felipe knew what he was talking about and didn't send me riding a cold trail."

For an hour or more he sat smoking and watching, but nothing happened. The lower edge of the sun was close to the crests of the western peaks and soon it would be dark. Hatfield began to think that, after all, Felipe might have been mistaken, although he knew the scout usually knew whereof he spoke.

And then without any preliminary warning it came. Smoke was rising in the foothills of the Chisos, west by slightly south of the ridge. A tall, slender column shot into the sky, broke at its base, drew slowly upward into space and melted from view. A rolling ball-like puff followed, exploding into the air like a bursting bomb. Again came a slender spiral, then another puff, and another. Another thin column followed, and a series of puffs. Columns and puffs shimmered darkly in the sunshine as they wrote their ominous message across the sky.

Hatfield could not read the mysterious dots and dashes — no white man could, the Indians keep their secret well — but he knew they constituted a telegraph code as clear and precise as anything that ever went over the whispering wires.

He knew that down there in the west, atop some beetling cliff, a half-clad Comanche, eagle feather slanting low in his dirty white turban, necklace of bear claws about his sinewy neck, was deftly manipulating a blanket or a deer hide over a blaze smothered with green stuff. Alternately imprisoning and releasing the rolling smoke, sending it upward in the form he desired and by so doing, sending a message to keen eyes that watched amid the hills below the Rio

Grande.

The smoke column thinned and vanished after a last burst of puffs. The clear blue of the Texas sky was unstained. The peaceful gold of the dying sunlight again washed crag and bench and towering mountain wall.

Hatfield turned his gaze toward the mysterious purple hills to the south. His eyes narrowed slightly as the soaring vault above the shadowy pinnacles remained clear and undefiled. The minutes passed, the sun sank lower, an utter hush seemed to blanket the earth. Hatfield sat tensely in his saddle, his glance never shifting. Abruptly he relaxed; a low exclamation of satisfaction passed his lips.

Smoke was rising from the hills to the south. The fantastic dance of the shifting vapors repeated, with variations. Hatfield's black brows drew together and the concentration furrow between them deepened. His eyes measured the distance from one signal post to the other.

"Twenty miles as the crow flies," he muttered speculatively, "and even Pedro Cartina hasn't got wings. Nigh onto thirty, the way he'll have to travel; but he'll travel fast."

He swung about and gazed westward into the red blaze of the sun that still showed above the peaks, and shook his head.

"More than thirty miles to the Post," he mused. "Thirty miles back, and time for the boys to get ready. No, as I told Felipe, it can't be done. I've got to play a lone hand. Hell of a chance to take, but I'm not likely to get another opportunity like this. Dropping a loop on Cartina is like trying to rope a rattlesnake sliding for its hole. You sure have to get the breaks. Maybe this is it. Cartina has gotten his smoke signal and answered it. Which means the stage is set for action and the representatives of the tribes — Yaquis, Creeks, Apaches, and others — have assembled at Kepnau's village for the council. Give Cartina a chance to talk to them and he'll swing them in line and there'll be such an uprising along the Border as Texas has never seen. Which of course is just what Anton Page wants, and what Tom Weston thinks he wants. Well, one man against a hundred is long odds, but sometimes things work out to even up. Cartina and his men should cross the Rio Grande shortly after dusk, and with the river up like it is there's just about one place where they can make it — the Vegas ford. Then they'll follow the Vegas trail and turn off somewhere on a track that leads to Kepnau's village. Let's go, horse, we've got to make the Vegas ford before dark."

Goldy answered with a snort, tossed his black mane and moved swiftly down the sag. Under the sun's rays his glossy hide looked like burnished copper with mane and tail of shredded ebony.

Hatfield pushed back his broad-brimmed "J.B." and ran slender fingers through his black hair. His forehead was strikingly white in contrast to his deeply bronzed cheeks. He hitched his double cartridge belts a little higher about his lean waist, the black butts of the heavy Colts in their carefully worked and oiled cut-out holsters flaring out from his sinewy hips. As is the habit of men who ride much alone, he talked to his horse, his voice low and deep, with a peculiar vibrant note threading the even tones —

"Unless I've forgotten, feller, a bit over to the east from the foot of this sag is a big, dry wash that runs nearly down to the ford. The sides should be well grown up with octillos and mescal plants and weeds to provide good cover. When we get to the end of the wash we should be able to hear anybody crossing the ford. We'll let the buzzards pass and then we'll try and trail 'em. After that it will be mostly luck and hoping for the breaks. If we get them, maybe we'll have Cartina and put a nice tangle in *Senor* Page's twine."

Although he didn't mention it, Hatfield knew that the alternative might well be a lonely grave beneath the cathedral arches of the hills where the white yucca blossoms sway like swung censers and the golden blooms of the mescal explode into sky-freed stars.

The shadows were turning from hard black to misty purple when the golden horse rounded a corner of the wash and the distant-faint shimmer of the Rio Grande showed through a tangle of scanty foliage. Hatfield pulled him to a walk and finally halted him in a thicket where a thread of water purled from under a shelving stone and there was a rich carpet of grass. He slipped the bit and allowed the sorrel to graze.

A lonely little wind wandered up from the south, murmuring to itself as it breasted the swelling rampart of the hills. It was a silent wind and distant sounds traveled far on its velvet wings.

In and out between the vortices of moving air weaved a tiny clicking. Hatfield might well have been excused if he had translated it as the mandibles of some insect rubbing against each other or as the kiss of branch on branch amid the mesquite. It was a persistent little sound that, apparently, grew no louder.

Small as it was, however, it brought Hatfield erect from the trunk against which he had been lounging. Silently he glided to where Goldy stood with attentively cocked ears. One hand closed lightly over the velvety muzzle, the other soothingly stroked the sleek neck.

"Can't take chances on you getting a notion to sing a little song to the evening star," he breathed. Goldy was usually a very silent horse, but equine nature is sometimes as perverse as its human counterpart. A single neigh or even a loud snort at the present moment might have been a signed death warrant for the sorrel's rider.

Steadily the rhythmic clicking grew in volume, though never becoming very loud. Suddenly it ceased, was echoed by a faint splashing.

Silent, almost, as the motionless shadows along the river bank a troop of moving shadows drifted over the dark water. They reached the near bank, clambered up it and in ghostly procession clicked-clacked past the mouth of the draw.

Hatfield counted a dozen or more of mounted men. He waited until the last of the group had passed his hiding place; then he swung into the saddle and gathered up the reins.

"Okay, feller," he told Goldy. "They're riding the Vegas trail and they'll keep following it until they come to a track that leads to Kepnau's village, wherever that is. It's up to us to hold their trail."

Ghost-like, the great sorrel drifted down the wash, a little later following a trail that paralleled the draw and sloped inward. Swiftly they climbed under a paling sky.

They entered the vestibule of the hills as a great white moon soared up from behind the eastern crags and flooded the scene with silver light. Hatfield kept in the shadow at the edge of the trail, peering and listening. Twice he sighted the quarry, a considerable distance ahead, breasting the rise. He felt sure he could spot the turning-off spot and kept well in the rear. Where a wide bench levveled off beneath the slopes, he pulled the horse to a walk and leaned forward in an attitude of tense listening. He could hear the faint clicking ahead; then abruptly it stilled.

"Turned off," he muttered and quickened Goldy's pace. His keen eyes searched the growth on the left. He had covered less than a quarter of a mile when he discerned a dark opening in the chaparral. It was a narrow track that wound westward through growth. He turned into it and again slowed the sorrel. Another thousand yards and a faint murmuring came to his ear. A moment later he smelled wood smoke. Then light flickered through the trees. He pulled Goldy to a halt and considered the situation. Directly ahead was the Comanche village.

He slanted the horse off the trail and along a gentle slope that paralleled it and was clumped with chaparral thickets. When the glow amid the trees was directly opposite and above, he dismounted, let the split reins fall to the ground and drifted away silently on foot.

He could see by the flooding moonlight that to the west was a dizzily steep, boulder-strewn fall into the dark depths of an arroyo. Above was a level bench flanked by a bristle of cottonwoods where sprawled a small Comanche village, one of the flimsy temporary communities the fierce nomads of the plains erected from time to time until the restless urge sent them moving onward.

A council fire burned brightly on an open space and about the fire were grouped several score Indians and a sprinkling of swarthy Mexicans. Hatfield recognized lean hawk-nosed Yaquis from south of the Rio Grande, broad-faced Apaches, almost black in coloring, lighter Kiowas and lean, bold-eyed Comanches. It appeared that representatives of all the Border Tribes were present, drawn together by urgent purpose or some master-mind that quieted for the time the feud always smoldering between these natural enemies. Such a gathering was ominous and boded no good for the Border.

Standing outlined against the blaze was a very tall, broad-shouldered man with dark eyes glowing in the shadow of his sombrero. The firelight glinted on the reddish beard that grew high on his swarthy cheeks.

"Cartina!" breathed Hatfield. "Yes, it's Cartina; I'd know those red whiskers anywhere — mighty seldom you see them that color on a Mexican, even one of predominant Spanish blood."

A second figure, even taller than the bearded man and swathed in a blanket that came almost to his eyes was speaking, his voice muffled by the blanket's folds. The bearded man and the others about the fire were giving him their undivided attention.

"Important tribal chief or a medicine man," Hatfield decided. "To heck with him! Cartina is the big skookum he-wolf of the pack. After the pow-wow is over, he'll tell them what to do. That sidewinder sure has got something, all right, if he can get such a bunch together and keep them from using their knives on one another."

With steady eyes he calculated the group about the fire. His glance wandered to the trail stretching eastward. The space between the tree trunks was broad, but shadowy under the spreading branches. Above was the beetling rise of the cliffs, unclimbable by even a mountain goat. Below stretched the gentle slope bathed in the moonlight. And as he surveyed the terrain, Hatfield formulated a daring plan that he believed might work. He shook his head and his eyes turned to the west where the ragged lip of the bench plummeted dizzily into the black arroyo.

"It looks like plain damn foolishness," he muttered, "but it's a chance — a chance to break this thing up before it gets going good, a chance to save hundreds of killings. Well, here goes!"

He turned and made his way back softly down the slope, his lips set so tight a ripple of muscle showed along his lean jaw.

Mounting Goldy, he rode back east, slanting up the slope until he reached the trail on the bench. Unhesitatingly he wheeled the sorrel and rode toward the village among the cottonwoods, loosening his guns in their holsters.

4.

In the Indian village, the red-bearded man still stood outlined in the blaze of the council fire, listening to the words of the blanketed speaker. From time to time the squatting Comanches and Apaches grunted gutturally. The lean Mexicans hissed approbation. The sinister Yaquis, most deadly of all, said nothing, but their beady eyes gleamed.

Suddenly one seated in the outer fringe of the firelight turned his head and slanted his ear to the east. Other heads came around. The blanketed man ceased his harangue. The red-bearded man tensed, peering uncertainly through the blaze of the fire. Then, in a whirling instant, all was confusion.

From the aisle between the cottonwoods burst a roar of gunfire. Red flashes stabbed the shadows; bullets whistled past the heads of the panicked Indians. There was a thunder of hoofs, a shape loomed gigantic in the uncertain light, rushing toward the council fire.

To the wildly scattering group it seemed that a score of yelling, shooting horsemen were charging them. With one accord, Mexican, Comanche, Apache and Yaqui dived for cover. The blanketed figure boomed something inarticulate. The red-bearded man yelled commands and his hands flashed to his guns. Before he could grip them, the charging horseman was upon him, leaping the crackling fire, scattering burning embers far and wide.

The tall figure leaned from the saddle. Fingers like rods of nickel steel gripped the bearded man's velvet collar. A mighty heave and he was hauled across the front of the high Mexican saddle, the big pommel jabbing him in the pit of the stomach and knocking the breath out of him. For a pain-blazing instant he was dazed.

"Trail, Goldy, trail!" roared his captor.

A gun blazed from the shadows and Hatfield felt the burn of a bullet along his bronzed cheek. Then he was beyond the fire, with a crackle of shots behind him and the whistle of slugs about his ears. A pandemonium of yells in half a dozen different dialects rang through the night; and the thud of running feet.

"Take it, Goldy!" Hatfield shouted as the ragged lip of the bench fell away under the sorrel's very nose.

Goldy took it. Snorting and blowing, the stones rolling under his irons, he went down the slope, keeping his feet by a miracle of ability, leaping over boulders, swerving around clumps of brush.

Guns roared from the lip above. Howls of rage rose to the stars. The Indian village seethed and sputtered like an over-boiling pot. But the golden horse and his rider were already a shadow among the shadows. Another instant and they vanished from the sight of those above.

The red-bearded man had recovered his faculties and was fighting like a wildcat. He managed to get one gun from its holster, only to have it knocked clattering from his hand. He twisted about and lunged at his captor's face.

The blow was blocked before it had traveled six inches and the next instant a fist like a block of iron crashed against his jaw. With a muffled groan he went limp. Hatfield gave a satisfied grunt and bent all his attention to keeping the plunging horse from turning a somersault that would land all three in the middle of next week.

Gradually he steadied the frantic horse, guided him and brought him panting and blowing to the flat floor of the arroyo. Through the shadowy dark he sent him at a gallop, glancing over his shoulder from time to time, listening intently for sounds of pursuit.

The arroyo was widening. Moonlight

seeped into it, graying the shadows, changing blurred edges to clean-cut outlines. The sides fell away still further and silver beams poured down from a sky like frost-sprinkled velvet. The silence remained unbroken.

Hatfield pulled Goldy to a walk, knotted the reins and let them drop onto his arching neck; he turned his captive over. The fellow was groaning with returning consciousness.

The Lone Wolf suddenly stiffened, leaned forward, an expression of incredulity flitting across his bronzed face. He swore a bewildered and disgusted oath. He stared at the dark countenance over which the moonlight was pouring in a revealing flood. The eyelids were flickering and an instant later they opened and burning dark eyes stared upward with a dazed expression.

It was not the eyes that riveted Hatfield's attention. They were all right. But the red beard certainly was not. It was tucked up under the captive's ear, its peaked point at a grotesque angle with the chin.

With another oath, Hatfield gripped it, pulled it free and revealed lean, swarthy cheeks and straight thin lips without suspicion of a hair on them. He slipped lithely from the saddle, carrying the captive with him as easily as if he were a child and set him on his feet.

The fellow swayed for an instant, then steadied himself. A white-toothed grin fleeted across his face and his dark eyes snapped.

"Buenos noches, Senor Ranger!" he drawled in soft Spanish. Hatfield looked down at him from his great height.

"Feller," he said pleasantly, "who the hell are you and what do you mean going around wearing red whiskers and looking like Pedro Cartina?"

The captive chuckled throatily.

"I am one of several," he explained, "who dress as does *El Gran Generale,* even to the *barba roja,* the red beard, to protect him from just such dangers as threatened him tonight."

"I see," Hatfield nodded. "That's why you stood out in the light where everybody could see you; and that fellow wrapped up in a blanket was Cartina, eh?"

"Si, Teniente Hatfield."

The Lone Wolf's eyes narrowed a little. "How the devil do you know I'm Hatfield?" he demanded. "Where did you ever see me before?"

The swarthy prisoner shrugged with Latin expressiveness. "Never before have I seen you. But who else, even of the Texas Rangers, but *Capitan* McDowell's lieutenant would dare what you dared tonight?"

Hatfield nodded, the suspicion of a smile twitching his firm lips. "Yes, I'm Hatfield," he admitted. "And you?"

"I am Doroteo Arango, mostly called Pancho," the other replied. "Though not for long, I think," he added with grim humor.

The Ranger eyed him speculatively, his glance flickering over the gun that still remained in its holster and centering at length on the fancily stitched high-heeled boots.

"I figure you'll have sore feet before you've gone very far in those *botas,*" he predicted, "but I reckon you can make it across the River."

The Mexican youth stared at him uncomprehendingly. "You — you mean, *Teniente,* that you are going to let me go free?" he ventured at last.

"Reckon that's right," Hatfield admitted. "You seem to be a decent sort, and I've got a notion there's the making of a man in you. Where are you from?"

"From Durango, *Teniente,* far to the south."

"Go back there. Steer clear of men like Cartina and their schemes. Yes, I know, many of you young fellows think he is *un*

62

gran generale and *Mejico*'s liberator. He's not. He's just a murdering bandit out to feather his own nest. It's not much of a man that hides under a blanket and has a youngster stand out in the light to get what *he* ought to be willing to take his chances on. Ever look at it that way? Someday a man will arise, a man of the people, who will free Mexico from the 'Cartinas' in high places, but he won't be the Cartina sort." He paused, then continued in friendly tones —

"All right, get going. You still have one gun and you ought to be able to find a horse the other side of the Line. I haven't time to fool with you — got a fifty-mile ride ahead of me back to the Post. And besides," he added with a whimsical grin that flashed his even teeth startlingly white against his bronzed cheeks and made his stern face wonderfully pleasant, "after attempting to bring in the big skookum he-wolf of the pack, I don't feel like settling for a cub, even if it does appear to come from a prize litter."

He swung lithely into the saddle and turned the golden horse's nose to the west.

"Adios, muchacho!" he smiled down at the lad.

The young Mexican hesitantly extended a dark hand. The Ranger's steely grip crushed the tapering fingers with friendly force. Then the sorrel's irons clicked over the prairie.

The Mexican boy stood staring after horse and rider until they merged with the shadows and vanished. Slowly he turned toward where the Rio Grande flowed jet and silver between banks of pearly gray.

"*He* would not hide his face from Death's own stare," he declared with conviction.

5.

Anton Page was pacing the plain whitewashed room that served him for an office, as was his wont when his activities were for a moment curbed or there was something on his mind; and every few minutes he would glance at the clock on the wall.

Page was a big man of imposing build. His square, close-cropped head, his large features, his alert eyes were those of a fighter. His mouth was a hard line that could set tight in merciless ferocity.

Suddenly he cocked his head in an attitude of listening. A horse was clicking up the gravel drive that led from the trail to the spacious ranchhouse. It halted in front of the building with a popping of saddle leather and a jingle of bridle irons. Page turned toward the door, expectantly. He flung it open as a knock sounded.

The man who stepped in was very tall, broad-shouldered, strikingly handsome with black hair, cameo-perfect features and glittering dark eyes. He wore a short peaked beard of a reddish hue that grew high up on his lean cheeks. His habitual expression was one of wise and sardonic amusement, as if he laughed at everything in life, including himself. He nodded to the ranch owner, dropped into a chair and deftly rolled a corn husk cigarette.

"Cartina, you're late," Page said, glancing irritably at the clock.

The other lighted his cigarette and drew in a lungful of smoke. He expelled it slowly.

"Lucky to be here at all," he remarked.

Page snorted with impatience. "Well?" he said.

"Well, Page?"

"Well, what have you accomplished?" Page asked, his irritation increasing. "What about the chiefs? Are they lined up?"

Pedro Cartina blew out more smoke. "Oh, the chiefs," he replied carelessly, "the chiefs are out in the Chisos foothills chasing moonbeams."

Page's jaw sagged a little. He stared at the bandit leader.

"What in the hell are you talking about?" he demanded.

"Oh, nothing much," Cartina answered, "except your *amigo* Jim Hatfield arrived at just the right time, busted up the council, carried off a fool dressed to look like me, and scared the blue blazing hell out of everybody. The chiefs are all trying to run him down, but they might as well try to drop a loop on a moonbeam, for all the good it will do them. He's quite a hombre, *Senor* Hatfield."

Anton Page raised both clenched fists above his head and swore till his face was purple. Cartina watched the exhibition with mild interest.

"You'll go off in a spell like that some day," he predicted, which, not unnaturally did not improve Mr. Page's temper. He spat out a few more expletives dealing with Jim Hatfield's ancestry and his probable destination, as viewed by Anton Page. Suddenly he ceased and dropped into a chair behind his desk.

"Will you please give me the details?" he requested, very quietly.

Cartina gave them, laconically. Page swore some more. Cartina fingered his beard.

"I really think I'll have to dye my whiskers," he commented with apparent irrelevance. "They appear to make me too damn conspicuous."

"I don't see why the hell you wear 'em anyhow," snorted Page.

"Oh, they impress the Indians," Cartina explained. "There's a legend among the Border Tribes — funny how it runs through all the tribes, doubtless of Aztec origin — a legend that the Thunder-god had a beard the color of the setting sun, and it prophesies that there will come a man with a red beard who will unite the tribes and lead them to conquest and victory. The fool Indians half believe it and a red beard impresses them. Juan Flores had one, and it helped him raise plenty of hell along the Border. You don't often see a Mexican with one."

"Mexican, hell!" snorted Page. "You're about as much a Mexican as I am."

"Oh, I have a little Spanish blood, and a little more Yaqui," Cartina returned. "Enough to darken my skin a bit. I get by."

Page returned to the original subject under discussion.

"So Hatfield made a fool out of you, too, eh?" he remarked.

"Too?"

"Yes. The other night Tom Weston dropped a loop on him and had him drug up to his ranchhouse. He gave him the choice of joining with him or be shot at sunrise, or some such theatrical nonsense."

"And what did Hatfield do?"

"What did he do? Walked out through a locked door and rode off on old Tom's pet saddle horse, with lead whistling all around him. Seems the bullet isn't run that can kill him!"

"I'll make a test of that before long," Cartina observed his face suddenly grim.

"No, you won't," Page instantly countered. "He's more valuable to us alive than dead."

Cartina stared at the other as if convinced he was suddenly bereft of his senses.

"Kill Hatfield, and another law skunk of the same sort will rise up to take his place," Page continued. "Things work out that way, and killing him is liable to do more harm than good. Public opinion is a funny thing — it blows with the wind — and Hatfield as a martyr to duty would very likely crystallize it against us right now at a time when it is veering in our direction. But Hatfield discredited, shown to be in cahoots with what's called the outlaw element, would be another matter. Hatfield is the outstanding Ranger, a symbol, as it were. Shown as something altogether different from what he sets up to be, he'd still be a symbol — a symbol of Ranger treachery and subversiveness, something for us to really hammer on. I've figured out a little plan that I believe will work. I've already laid the foundation."

"Let's hear about it," Cartina suggested.

Page drew his chair to the end of the desk. He leaned forward and spoke in a voice that, by dint of long practice, carried but a few feet. As the scheme unfolded, Cartina's eyes snapped.

"It might work," he conceded thoughtfully, when Page paused, expectant. "Yes, it might work. Just blamed foolish enough *to* work. That is, if there isn't some fool slip-up on somebody's part."

"There won't be," Page insisted confidently. "I've picked my men with the greatest care. And I've worked out every smallest detail. I think you'd better ride up and see Weston and do a little spade work with him, sort of prepare him for what's going to happen. What happened the other night must have given him something of a jolt. As I gather, it is pretty sure that Hatfield had a little inside assistance in escaping. Weston is already suspicious of nearly everybody. Perhaps he may have grown a bit suspicious of Hatfield and his motives. What he tried was a piece of foolishness, anyhow. I've a notion he realizes it, now. So go up and see him."

"I will," Cartina replied cheerfully. "Like to visit there."

"Sweet on old Tom's niece, eh? Sooner or later, women will be your ruination, as they have been for many another man."

"I know how to handle 'em," Cartina returned. He reached down and tapped the cruel spur on his heel with the heavy quirt he carried.

"With women and horses, nothing like a good spur and a good lash," he said. "I can use both, if necessary."

Page grunted and changed the subject. "I've already started the wheels turning," he remarked. "My little plan should be developing quickly. I've a notion Hatfield is in for a surprise when he gets back to the Post, and for a greater one soon after. I'll need your help, of course. Just do as I tell you and don't go off half-cocked. If you keep your head, with my help, you will be able to topple old *El Presidente* off his perch and become the new dictator of Mexico."

"Yes, with your help," Cartina repeated thoughtfully. "That is, if you don't take a notion to doublecross me. You're capable of that, you know, if it should happen to suit your convenience; you're not bothered by ethics. But," he added pleasantly, "if you do, I'll shoot you, sure as I'm sitting here."

Page glared, but something in the glittering eyes of the man facing him gave him pause. He drummed on the desk with his thick fingers.

"Ethics do not enter into the matter," he said, adding ruminatively, "A certain famous and wise man once said to his colleagues, 'Gentlemen, we hang together or we hang separately.' That just about states the case in this instance. It's up to us to work together if we're both to get what we want."

"You've got something there," Cartina conceded. "And I think your little scheme is okay, too, up to a certain point. After that, I think a slug through the back of his head would be better."

"Never mind trying to think," said Page. "You provide the general cussedness and I'll furnish the brains."

"Oh, you've got brains, all right," nodded Cartina, "but don't forget, brains can be spilled!"

6.

"All steel and whipcord, the whole six-foot-four of him. I figure him to be the quickest man on the draw in all Texas, and what he shoots at he hits. And brains to go with it, which isn't always so with big, husky, quick-draw men."

That's how Captain Bill McDowell once summed up Jim Hatfield. Perhaps McDowell was thinking along the same lines when the Lone Wolf lounged into his office along about mid-morning. McDowell noted his torn shirt, slightly discolored left eye, the skinned knuckles of his right hand and the livid streak across one bronzed cheek.

"Hmmm! must have been a lively go while it lasted," he commented. "Saw Weston, eh? Must have been a bit of a disagreement."

"Yes, we didn't exactly agree." Hatfield smiled at him. He sat down, rolled a cigarette and proceeded to regale his chief with an account of his recent misadventures. When he had finished, Captain Bill swore wearily.

"The whole blamed Border country 'pears to have gone loco," he declared. "What with Tom Weston, Cartina and Anton Page, it's like living in a den of rattlesnakes and Gila monsters. You don't know which way to jump. And here's another one they just pulled out of the hat. They're establishing a Post over at Cibola, the county seat, twenty miles east of Sanders, and putting you in charge."

72

Hatfield stared. "Whose idea was that?" he wondered.

"Don't know," grunted Captain Bill. "The orders just came through from the Adjutant General. You're to report there at once. Better take time out for a bit of sleep, though. You look as if you needed it."

"Know who's assigned to the troop?" Hatfield asked. Captain Bill shook his head.

"Understand they're men drawn from all over the state," he replied. "Some from up in the Panhandle, others from the Nueces country and the Trinity. Picked men, I suppose. Cibola *is* about the hub of the trouble hereabouts. I figured everything needed could be handled from over here, but I reckon they know what they're about over to Austin. Anyhow, that's the order and we can't argue with it. Be seeing you."

Hatfield took Captain Bill's advice and went to bed. He awoke shortly after dark, ate a leisurely dinner and started his trip to Cibola with the moon. He was familiar with the trail and it would be cooler riding at night. As he rode, he pondered the sudden and unexpected development. What had occurred was not illogical, however. He knew that there was grave concern at the capital over recent developments in the Border country. Tom Weston's ambitions were well-known, and although officialdom was wont to discount their importance, still they were just another symptom of the unrest that was gripping the state. The organized farmers of the state, calling themselves the "Patrons of Husbandry," were waging a bitter conflict against railroad monopoly. Their Populist, or People's Party was a power in the state. The members held socialist camp meetings and aligned themselves against the large landowners as well as the railroads and other aggregations of capital. The big ranches resented the growing numbers and influence of the farmers and from that resentment had grown cattle wars, fence-cutting, rustling, shootings and not a few pitched battles. Looking askance at the farm movement, the big owners in retaliation organized what later became the Texas and Southwestern Cattle Raisers Association. Anton Page with his wealth, influence and string of newspapers spearheaded the move-ment and the honest ranch owners were misguided enough to consider him their champion. Page opposed the progressive governor who occupied the chair at the time. The big owners were suspicious of the governor's motives and this strengthened Page's position. Some owners made the mistake of hiring notorious gunfighters to ride patrol for them. These proceeded to get out of hand and cause more trouble. All of which proved remunerative to the outlaw element. The Texas Rangers were in effect the only enforcement body that had been able to keep something like law and order.

The most turbulent section was the country along the farflung Mexican border. Here even such fantastic schemes as Tom Weston's would bear watching. And the rising power of Pedro Cartina south of the Rio Grande was cause for grave concern.

So it was not unreasonable that the authorities at the capital would think it wise to establish additional Ranger Posts in the troubled area.

Hatfield reached Sanders at daybreak. He slept again for a few hours and continued on the last leg of his journey, reaching Cibola shortly after noon. Here he found that the officials at the capital had moved fast. A large building on the outskirts of the town had already been rented and fitted up to serve as a barracks. Later in the day his troop arrived, numbering eight. With one exception they were mature men, taciturn, hard-bitten, with an air of quiet efficiency. Hatfield decided they should prove a capable lot.

"Looks like they combed all the eastern Posts for salty gents," he mused. "Well, that's the sort needed down here."

The one exception was a fresh-faced young fellow named Billy Grant, who had been assigned from Captain Hughes's Post at Alice. Hatfield liked his looks and felt that he was good Ranger material.

The older men proved to be clannish. They quickly became acquainted with one another and formed a tight group, playing cards in their spare time, riding into town in a body and drinking together in the Cibola saloons. They had little intercourse with the townspeople and evidently were well satisfied with their own company. Hatfield, knowing the kind, thought it best to leave them to their own devices when they were off-duty.

As a consequence, young Grant, who did not exactly fit into the group, was thrown much in Hatfield's company. He quickly developed an intense admiration for the Lone Wolf. Hatfield decided he could be depended on in any emergency and went out of his way to instruct the young fellow in the best Ranger traditions.

It was Billy who brought the tip relayed by a friendly Kiowa, that Pedro Cartina planned a raid on the Sanders-Cibola stage.

Hatfield felt that there might very well be something to it. He knew the stage often packed valuable gold shipments from the Sanders mines to Cibola, which it took to the railroad for shipment to the Government assay offices.

"Where the Vegas trail joins the Cibola," he mused. "Sounds sort of reasonable. The Vegas is a straight shoot to Mexico. Yes, if the skunk has something in mind, right there is where he'd most likely make his try. A quick swoop and off to the Border before pursuit can be organized."

He thought of notifying the Sanders mine officials, even going so far as to write a letter with the intention of having Billy deliver it, then changed his mind. Here was a chance to drop a loop on the Border pest and eliminate him, and at the same time give old Tom Weston a jolt that might do some good. It would serve to shake Weston's complacent belief that Cartina was a patriot guided by only the highest motives and with the liberation and welfare of his people in mind. A liberator caught trying to rob a stage ceases to be an inspiration and is looked upon somewhat askance by even his most credulous believers.

The troop left the Post a little past midnight. At the moment of departure, young

Billy Grant turned up missing.

"Well, we can't wait for him," Hatfield decided. "We want to get all set by daylight. If those buzzards get there first, we may be in for a hot reception; it's a bad bunch."

"You can't depend on these young fellers," grumbled Sam Johnson, a grizzled borderman with an irascible disposition. "They're always skalleyhootin' off somewhere, getting mixed up with a *senorita* or something."

Hatfield thought it unlikely but he only nodded and ordered the troop under way. Johnson was still grumbling as they left Cibola.

"Betcha it turns out to be a cold trail," he remarked pessimistically to Hatfield.

"Could be," the Lone Wolf admitted, "but we can't afford to miss any bets."

"Guess that's right," Johnson agreed grimly. "Anyhow, it's all in a day's work, and I get tired of settin' around doing nothing."

The night was still and clear with sounds carrying a long way. Hatfield did not push the troop. They had plenty of time to reach their destination and by taking it easy they were less likely to miss something that might be of significance.

Nothing happened in the course of the ride, however, and shortly before dawn they holed up where the Vegas trail, winding up from the south, joined the broader Cibola.

A long and tedious wait followed, with nothing to break the monotony. The sun rose in scarlet and gold. Birds sang. A strengthening breeze shook down myriad sparkling dew gems from the grass heads. Little animals began going about the business of the day. The sun climbed higher, the heat increased. Flies bothered the horses and the silent watchers. The Vegas trail stretched white and empty. Several freight wagons rumbled past on the Cibola and a lone cowhand or two.

"Just a waste of time, this whole business," grumbled Johnson, glancing through the tangle of branches at the sun, which was nearing the zenith. "We — listen! here comes something."

Hatfield heard it, too, the clicking of hoofs and grind of tires beyond the bend in the Cibola to the west.

"That'll likely be the stage," whispered Johnson, edging his horse in close to Hatfield's mount. He was within arm's reach of the Lone Wolf when he tightened his grip on the reins. His right hand dropped stealthily to his gun butt.

All eyes were to the front. Johnson deftly drew his gun and clubbed it. The Vegas trail still stretched empty.

A moment later the Cibola stage bulged into view around the bend a couple of hundred yards to the west. A guard sat beside the driver, rifle cradled across his knees. Inside the stage, leaning out the windows, were several passengers. Nothing about the approaching vehicle hinted at disturbance of any kind.

"Yes, guess it was a cold trail, all right," Hatfield remarked over his shoulder to Johnson. "We'll ask them if they saw anything on the way over."

As the stage drew near, the troop rode out into the open, Johnson close beside Hatfield and a little to the rear.

Instantly the peaceful scene erupted into explosive action. The guard flung up his rifle and fired point-blank. Johnson's gun hand rose in a swift and accurate gesture. The tall form of Jim Hatfield reeled sideways and toppled to the ground to lie face downward, arms outstretched. From the ranks of the "Rangers" a shot rang out. The stage driver gave a choking cry and plummeted from his high perch to the dust of the trail. As half a dozen guns menaced him, the guard dropped his rifle and raised his hands. From inside the stage came the cries of startled passengers; white faces peered out the windows.

Old Johnson spoke, his voice harsh, menacing —

"Everybody out! and be careful what you do with your hands if you don't want the same thing *he* got. Parker, see if that buzzard killed the Boss. If Jim's dead, I'll let him have it!" His gun muzzle trained on the shaking guard.

Parker swung down from the saddle, knelt beside Hatfield.

"Just creased," he announced. "He'll be coming out of it in a little while."

"Okay," said Johnson. He gestured to the lined-up passengers with his gun muzzle.

"Empty your pockets, gents," he ordered. "Crane, you and Brady haul out the strongbox and load it on the horse. Move! before somebody comes along."

The stupefied passengers, their glances shifting from the menacing guns to Hatfield's prone form and back, obeyed orders. The strongbox was hauled out and loaded onto a horse led out of a nearby grove by a swarthy, beady-eyed man who had *not* been one of the Ranger group.

"Pick up the Boss and drape him over his saddle," Johnson ordered. "We're taking him along. He'll be all right in a little while." He turned to the stage guard who still sat motionless, his hands in the air.

"Grab those reins and get this shebang going," he said. "And don't stop, and don't look back. Inside, gents," he told the passengers. "Move!"

The orders were obeyed with alacrity. The guard plied the whip and sent the unwieldy coach careening down the trail toward Cibola. The group beside the trail faded into the brush. A few moments later they turned into the Vegas trail that led to Mexico. They rode swiftly for several miles. Then Johnson gestured to the limp form draped across Goldy's saddle.

"Take him into the brush and dump him," he said. "His horse will stay with him. He won't be coming out of it for quite a spell. I handed him a hefty wallop on the back of the head."

"I think it'd be better to put a slug through him," grumbled the man called Parker.

"Forget it!" Johnson said. "You know what Page's orders were, and we're doing just what he told us to do. Want to get into a row with him? Unhealthy business, feller."

"You're right about that," Parker admitted sullenly, "but just the same I figure it's a mistake. You fellers don't appreciate that big hellion. I do. Remember what I tell you, we're going to be sorry we didn't do him in. This thing ain't going to work out right. I got a feeling it ain't."

"You'll get another kind of feeling if you don't do what you're told," answered Johnson. "Okay, a hundred yards off the trail will be far enough. If somebody finds him it won't matter so much, but I don't think anybody will. He'll just put the rope around his own neck."

"There'll be a rope around somebody's neck before this thing is finished," growled the pessimistic Parker. "Mind what I tell you."

"Okay, croaker!" said Johnson. "Now let's get started. There'll be hell to pay when that stage gets into town. Hope that fool guard doesn't tangle his twine when they start asking him questions; but I reckon he won't. Heck knows he was coached often enough on what to say. Let's go! The sooner we're across the River and in Mexico the better *I'll* feel. Old Sheriff McCauley is a tough hombre and he ain't in on the deal. If he gets within shooting distance of us it's liable to be him who'll play the hand out. Let's go!"

7.

It was nearly dark when Jim Hatfield recovered consciousness. He groaned, thrashed about, finally struggling to a sitting position. His head was one vast ache and there was a crawling nausea in the pit of his stomach. For several moments he sat with his face in his hands, trying to gain control over the cloying faintness that threatened to sweep him back into oblivion. Finally, with trembling fingers, he fished the makin's from his shirt pocket and after several vain attempts, managed to roll and light a cigarette. After a few deep drags on the brain tablet, his nerves quieted somewhat, his stomach stopped turning somersaults and his head cleared a little. He looked dazedly about. He hadn't the slightest idea where he was or how he got there. And only the vaguest notion of what had happened. He raised a hand and gingerly felt of the sizable lump on the back of his head.

"Who in the blazes hit me, and why?" he wondered aloud. He recalled the upward fling of the stage guard's rifle, but nothing after that save a blaze of white light and a numbing pain. That he had been struck from behind was certain, but heck! only Johnson was close behind him. It didn't make sense. But the fact remained that he had been hit over the head, presumably with a gun barrel, and hit hard. And how the devil did he get out here in the brush, hours later?

No satisfactory answers to any of the questions presented themselves. He smoked the cigarette down to a stub and rolled another. His strength was coming back his brain clearing still more. After a little while he risked getting to his feet. He swayed dizzily for an instant, but the dizziness soon passed. He glanced about, remembered his horse, and a moment later saw him grazing contentedly nearby, shaking his head from time to time in an irritated fashion as the bit interfered with his chewing. Hatfield walked toward him unsteadily. Goldy raised his head with an inquiring snort.

"Decided to come out of it, eh?" the horse seemed to say. "Well, it's about time."

Hatfield regarded him in silence for a few moments, then —

"Too bad you can't talk and tell me what happened," he said. "Well, I reckon we'd better try and find out where we are, and a few other things."

His head had begun to clear and he remembered having been hit from behind. One of his own men must have struck him down, but why would any one of them do such a thing? He decided he'd better get back to the barracks and demand an accounting from each one. And the explanations had better be good, he told himself grimly. But first he had to find out where he was. He mounted Goldy, confident that the horse would make for home and a helping of oats, if he let him roam freely.

That was just what Goldy did. He forced his way purposefully through the brush and a few minutes later came out on a well traveled trail. Hatfield glanced about in the fast-fading light and spotted several landmarks that told him he must be on the Vegas trail and not far south of the Cibola. His view was corroborated when Goldy turned to the right. Hatfield let him choose his own gait. Ten minutes more and they came out on a second track that could only be the Cibola. Goldy turned right again. Almost instantly Hatfield recognized the spot where he and the troop had holed up.

"Well, we're headed for town," he muttered, "and we can't get there quickly enough to suit me." He settled himself in the saddle and quickened Goldy's pace.

It was long past dark when he saw the lights of Cibola winking through the gloom. The upper edge of the moon was just showing in the east and the shadows were taking on sharper outlines. Another twenty minutes and he was approaching the barracks. The building was dark save for a single light that burned in the room Hatfield used as an office. He pulled to a halt in front of the structure, walked to the front door and opened it. A chair scraped back and young Billy Grant leaped to his feet, his eyes wide with amazed unbelief.

"Jim!" he exclaimed. "My God! why did you come here?"

Hatfield dissembled his surprise. "Why not?" he asked as casually as he could.

"Why not! They say that driver is going to die! They'll hang you, sure as hell, if they catch you. They're looking for you now."

"None of the other boys here?"

"No! Do you think they're damn fools, too? The sheriff is trailing them. Jim, the men in that coach recognized you. I tell you they'll string you up if they get their hands on you."

Hatfield sat down and rolled a cigarette. "Billy," he said, "suppose you start at the beginning and tell me everything. Tell me just what those passengers in the coach said when they got to town."

Graham told him. Hatfield got an account of the hold-up, the shooting of the driver, the looting of the stage and the passengers and the stories they told when they got to town of him being creased by the guard's bullet and being packed off unconscious by his companions.

"Creased, eh?" Hatfield commented. "Billy did you ever see anybody creased by a bullet?"

"Why, yes," Graham replied.

Hatfield stood up and removed his hat. He turned around to show the lump on the back of his head.

"That look like a bullet crease?" he asked.

Graham peered at the swelling. "No," he admitted, "it doesn't. Looks more like you'd got walloped by a rock or a club."

"Or a gun barrel," Hatfield supplemented. "Now look my head over and see if you *do* see any signs of a crease anywhere."

Graham looked, and needless to say, found none.

"What in heck?" he sputtered.

"That's what I'd like to know," Hatfield replied. But he was beginning to see a glimmer of light on the matter.

"By the way," he asked suddenly, "where were you when we started out last night? Why weren't you with us?"

Graham looked astonished. "Why, I was delivering that letter to the manager of the

Sanders Mining and Smelting Company," he replied.

"What letter?"

"The letter you wrote and gave to Johnson to give me to take to Sanders," Graham said.

"I see," Hatfield nodded. "Only catch in it is I didn't give any letter to Johnson. Well, Billy, what do you think about it all?"

For an instant Hatfield saw doubt cloud the young fellow's eyes, but it almost instantly cleared away. Grant spoke unhesitantly —

"Jim, there's enough evidence against you to hang you, if they catch you. Never mind what I ought to think. I'm *telling* you to ride, and ride fast. Get the heck away from here before somebody sees you. Go to Mexico — any place. I don't know what the heck's going on, but you're on the spot."

Hatfield thought that a fine example of understatement. He was silent for a moment, his mind working swiftly, the vague outlines of a plan forming in his alert brain.

"Billy," he said at length, "I think you're giving me good advice, and I'm going to take it. First I want to fill up my saddlebags with a little chuck and a few cooking utensils, and get me a blanket. I figure to need 'em. And I'd like to ask a favor of you. Ride over to the Post at Franklin and tell Captain

McDowell everything you know. And tell him I said I'd be seeing him, at the right time. Don't forget."

"I won't," Graham promised as he hurried to get the blanket and help Hatfield assemble some staple provisions, a small flat bucket and a little skillet, all an old campaigner needed to make himself comfortable in the open.

Hatfield met several men as he rode out of town, but although one or two paused to stare, none accosted him. He followed the Cibola trail for about two miles and then turned off into a faint track, less than a game trail, that wound into the higher hills. He had little fear of pursuit but he wanted to find a place where he could hole up comfortably to think and plan. Just as dawn was streaking the sky with bars of tremulous rose, he came upon a shallow cave at the base of a cliff. The spot was elevated and gave a good view in every direction. A trickle of water seeped from under the cliff nearby. He lighted a small fire and soon had an appetizing meal prepared, with plenty of steaming coffee. After eating he lighted a cigarette and stretched out on a bed of leaves to consider the situation in general.

It did not take long to see the hand of Anton Page in the affair. And Hatfield experienced a sudden new respect for the publisher's devilish ingenuity. He did not discount the seriousness of the predicament in which he found himself. But in addition to the blow to his own reputation was something infinitely more important, as he saw it. The Ranger corps was abruptly fighting for its life as a law enforcement organization. Already Page would have his presses rolling and Hatfield could visualize the streams of vituperation and slander that would pour forth.

"Yes, a cute scheme," he mused. "Used his influence, and perhaps Tom Weston's also, to get the new Post established. Then slid in his own men. Must have been working on the scheme for quite a while. Infiltrated the Posts over east with them and then negotiated the transfers when he was ready to strike. Yes, a cute scheme, but, although doubtless he doesn't realize it, in one way he slipped. He's laid himself wide open. Those lizards will have to keep under cover, now, and sooner or later *they'll* slip. Very seldom do you find one of the owlhoot breed who won't spill his guts to save his own neck when he gets in a tight place. Guess it's my business to see that some of them get in a tight place. And it shouldn't be so difficult. If Page doesn't keep a close rein on them, they'll bust somewhere. And I've a notion, too, that I sort of tangled his twine for him, with the help of Billy Grant. Easy to see that he figured I'd go barging into town when I got my senses back and get myself clapped in the calaboose. Then I'd have been so busy trying to get myself out of the jam I wouldn't have had time to devote to *Senor* Page. Now that I'm on the loose I figure he'll start his bunch trying to run me down. That's just what I want to happen. But if they get a whack at me, it won't be a lick on the back of the head with a gun barrel next time. It'll be the hot end of a bullet. Page undoubtedly figured I'd be worth more alive, discredited and locked up, but now he'll know the only thing he can do is eliminate me. Well, I'll take my chances on that. It's been tried before, by experts. And I've got a mighty good hunch that Pedro Cartina will be mixed up in the deal, too. And Cartina suffers from prominence. He can hardly make a move without a good many folks knowing about it. Which doesn't hurt where I'm concerned. Yes, Page took a trick, all right, but the game isn't over till all the cards are down. Then we'll see who scoops the pot."

Well satisfied with the outcome of his reflections, he made a bed of dry leaves beside the fire, stretched out with his blanket over him and his saddle for a pillow and was soon fast asleep.

8.

Seated in his spacious living room, old Tom Weston read the latest edition of Anton Page's principal organ, *The Clarion.* Across the table from him sat his niece. Sylvia Mayfield, her slender fingers twining and untwining nervously.

UNMASKED AT LAST

screamed a black headline. There followed a lurid and gloating account of the Cibola stage robbery, sprinkled with fulminations against the Rangers in general and Jim Hatfield in particular. Old Tom read the article from beginning to end. Then he laid the paper down and looked at his elderly range boss who was lounging near the door smoking a cigarette.

"Curtis," old Tom said, "I don't believe it!"

Sylvia's fingers stopped moving. In her big eyes was a sudden glad light.

"Nope, I don't believe it," Weston repeated. "I talked with that young feller and I figure I've lived long enough to be a pretty good judge of men and their motives. He's honest as the day is long. He was willing to face loaded rifles for his principles and beliefs."

A cloud of doubt suddenly dimmed the strangely brilliant blue eyes.

"He *believed* he was right," said old Tom, as if arguing the point with himself. "And he was ready to die for what he thought right. Nope, I don't believe it."

"There are other folks who don't believe it, either," said Curtis, taking a long drag on his cigarette. "Remember that young Mexican feller you hired the other day? The one with the white grin and packs two guns?"

"Uh-huh, I liked his looks," nodded Weston. "Let's see, what was his name?"

"Pancho Arango," Curtis said. "Well, he was in town with me today. We were in the Golconda saloon, having a drink. You know — the one Pete Rader runs."

"An unsavory character," interpolated old Tom.

Curtis nodded agreement. "Well, Pete was sounding off big to anybody who would listen to him. He 'lowed the Rangers were all a bunch of owlhoots and ended up by saying Jim Hatfield was the orneriest skunk of the lot. Pancho had been listening without saying a word, only those funny-colored eyes of his kept getting shinier and shinier. When Pete had finished his cussin' and rarin', Pancho tapped him on the shoulder. '*Senor,*' he said, real soft and pleasant-like, '*Senor,* you lie!' "

"Huh?"

"Yes, that's just what he said, soft and easy, but loud enough for everybody in the room to hear. Well, Pete swelled up like a pizened steer.

" 'Why, you goldarn oiler!' he yells, and up went his fist. He's got one the size of a ham."

"And —" prompted Weston, leaning forward in his interest.

"Pancho hit him. And Boss, I'd never have believed a man could be hit that hard. Pete weighs better'n two hundred, I reckon, but he just rose up off the floor like he'd all of a sudden growed wings. He went clean across a table and landed on the floor with his head in a spittoon and stayed there. Pancho looked around the room, with his thumbs hooked over his cartridge belts, and he was grinnin', only the sort of tooth-showing grin a mountain lion wears before he gets down to business."

"And then what happened?" Weston asked.

"Nothing happened," Curtis replied.

"Nobody said a word, nobody moved a hand, which was damn sensible, I'd say. Pancho turned around and walked out."

"Hmmm!" said old Tom. "Raise Pancho Arango's wages five dollars a month."

He reached for his pipe, filled it with black tobacco and after he got it drawing good, remarked:

"Wonder what became of Hatfield? Do you think the buzzards killed him?"

Sylvia stiffened in her chair, her eyes wide.

"Nope, they didn't kill him," Curtis replied. "Heck knows why they didn't, if it really was a frame-up. He was seen riding out of town right after dark. Couple of fellers swore it was him, all right. Came from the direction of the barracks. Understand the sheriff like to blew up when he heard about it when he got in toward daylight, after riding clean down to the Border and back. He got a little rest and lit out again. Said he'd run him down this time or know the reason why."

"Calc'late he'll have quite a few reasons to give, and that'll be all," grunted old Tom, glancing toward Sylvia, who had relaxed once more.

"By the way, Curtis," he added, "if you happen to get a line where Hatfield is, and maybe you can, send him word that I want to talk to him. That I want him to come here as my guest. As my guest, understand. Reckon you know what that means."

"Reckon I do," admitted Curtis as he lounged out. Old Tom puffed on his pipe and apparently sank into a reverie. He did not seem to notice when Sylvia quietly took her departure, except for a slight twinkle in his keen old eyes.

Pancho Arango was replacing a broken corral post when Sylvia approached him. He removed his sombrero and bowed with courtly grace.

"Pancho," Sylvia began without preamble, "you know Jim Hatfield, don't you?"

Arango bowed again reverently. "I am so honored," he replied.

"Do you think you can find him?" the girl asked.

Pancho glanced at her keenly, hesitated a moment, then —

"Doubtless."

"Find him!" the redheaded girl urged. "My uncle wants to talk to him. Find him, but bring him to me first. Will you do it, Pancho, for me?"

Pancho regarded her gravely, an inscrutable look in his dark eyes.

"It is the order," he said quietly.

Sylvia hesitated a moment. "Many men

are searching for him," she said at length. "Do you think they will catch him?"

This time Pancho Arango's smile was a grin. He abandoned his precise mission-school English and broke into the flowery idiom of the land of *manana.*

"Let them set their snares amid the mists of the mountain tops!" he said. "Or fly on the wings of the morning wind! Or walk the path of the moonbeams to where the River of Time runs over the edge of the world! *Then* will they catch *El Lobo Solo,* perhaps!"

9.

Meanwhile, there was a meeting in Anton Page's ranchhouse office. Page was in a towering rage. He hurled insults at the seven perturbed men who stood in front of his desk.

"Yes, you fumbled it," he stormed. "He *didn't* ride into town and get thrown in jail. I don't know how you did it, but you fumbled it somehow."

"But, Boss, we obeyed orders to the letter," protested Sam Johnson. "I knocked him out just as Ballard, the guard, pulled trigger. We packed him away from the trail and left him, with his horse beside him.

That's what you told us to do, and we did it."

"Well, you slipped somehow and he caught on," Page insisted. "He rode into town all right, slid in after dark, and slid out again. And the next morning young Grant was seen riding west like the devil beating tanbark. *He* was heading for the Post at Franklin to tell Bill McDowell whatever Hatfield told him to tell, you can bet on that."

"I thought it was a mistake in the first place, letting young Grant into the outfit," the pessimistic Parker observed querulously.

"I agree with you on that," snapped Page, "but that wasn't my doing. His father is one of the Adjutant General's friends and he was assigned to the Cibola Post by his office. I couldn't very well protest it. I'd already pulled wires in every direction to establish that Post and have you stupid fools assigned to it. I thought the seven of you would have brains enough to handle him. Guess I was mistaken. Well, no matter how it happened, you fumbled the chore and Jim Hatfield's on the loose."

"Don't see why he didn't give himself up," complained Parker. "You know and I know that when it came to a showdown he'd have beat the charge. No cow country jury would have convicted him."

"You damn fool!" exploded Page. "Can't you see why he didn't give himself up? Granted, he could likely have beaten the charge, although there would have always been a doubt left in men's minds, but not until after we'd accomplished what we set out to accomplish. He didn't give himself up because he caught on. He's out to get every one of you idiots, and everyone else concerned, if he can. Yes, he's on the loose, riding around through the hills, watching, listening, putting things together, waiting. Wonder if you've got brains enough to know what that means?"

A sudden stillness fell on the room, a stillness broken only by the lonely, hauntingly beautiful plaint of a hunting wolf. Parker shivered and muttered something incoherent.

Anton Page rasped an oath. He whirled his chair around and turned his gaze on Pedro Cartina, who lolled in a chair, an expression of sardonic amusement on his handsome, red-bearded face. Cartina seemed to be enjoying the situation, which tended to increase Page's anger.

"You'll laugh on the other side of your face if he happens to line sights with you," he predicted. "Don't forget, he's after you, too."

Cartina shrugged his broad shoulders. " 'Mountain shall never meet with mountain but at morning or even man shall meet again with man,' " he quoted lightly. "You wouldn't listen to me, Page, when I told you the right thing was to send a slug through the back of his head when you got the chance. Yes, he's on the loose, on his own and not hampered by regulations or restrictions. Nice prospect!"

One of Anton Page's outstanding characteristics was his ability to revert almost instantly from blazing anger to cold, calculating calm. Now he regarded Cartina speculatively, a gleam in his eyes.

"I think it *would* be a good notion for you to dye your whiskers," he said slowly. "With that and a bit of a mask you should get by. You're nearly a size to Hatfield, not quite so tall, not quite so broad, but on a horse the difference would hardly be noticed. All right, you've wanted to raid on this side of the Line for quite a while. I'm turning you loose. And I'm giving you these fools to work with. Hope they don't shoot you in the back. And as for *him,* we should be able to handle him without too much trouble. After all, he's just one man."

"Uh-huh, that's right, just one man," Cartina agreed dryly. "Just one man on his own. That's what he always was. Working alone is how he got his reputation. You know what they call him, the *Lone Wolf!*"

Once again there was an uneasy silence. And once again there came from the distant hills that weird, menacing plaint.

10.

Procrastination was not one of Pedro Cartina's besetting sins. He was not only ready to grasp Opportunity by the forelock, he could truthfully say, in the words of Napoleon, "Opportunity? I *make* opportunity!"

The long freight train had pulled into a siding to let the Sunrise Limited pass. Engineer, fireman and head brakeman were dozing comfortably in the engine cab, getting a little shut-eye overtime. They paid no attention to the two horsemen who came riding briskly along the trail that paralleled the right-of-way. Not even when the two riders pulled up beside the engine with a popping of saddle leather and a jingling of bridle irons did they rouse up beyond a casual glance. Cowboys stopping to inspect a locomotive were of too frequent occurrence to occasion comment. But when one of the riders dismounted, approached the hissing, grumbling locomotive and climbed the steps to the cab, they really opened their eyes — to look into the black muzzle of a gun.

"What in hell —" began the astonished engineer. The gunman cut him short.

"Shut up!" he said. "Straighten up and get hold of that throttle. You —" he gestured to the goggle-eyed brakeman — "get back and cut her loose. Move!"

A forward jut of the gun muzzle emphasized the command.

The brakeman didn't argue the point. He dropped down the steps with alacrity, and was immediately covered by another gun in the hand of the second rider. He hurried to the rear, jerked on the coupler lever.

"Give me a little slack!" he bawled to the engineer. The "hogger," grumbling and fuming, but acutely aware of the big Colt trained in his direction, threw over his reverse lever and cracked the throttle. The locomotive eased back. The brakeman jerked the lever, raising the coupling pin. "Okay!" he shouted.

The man in the cab gestured with his gun. The engineer muttered a curse, threw his reverse lever forward and cracked the throttle again. The engine moved forward, the couplers parted with a metallic jangle. The throttle slammed shut and the locomotive came to a halt, free from the train.

The man on the ground took over. "Go ahead and throw that switch and line up for the mainline," he told the brakeman.

"But good God, man!" the bewildered "shack" protested. "The Sunrise Limited will be along here in five minutes!"

The mounted man said nothing, but he cocked his gun suggestively. The brakeman hurried to obey orders. The target swung from white to red, the switch was open.

"All right, go ahead," the outlaw in the cab ordered.

The engineer saw there was no use to argue. "Okay," he said, "if you insist on getting us all killed. The Limited will knock this scrap heap into the next county."

"You let me worry about that," the other returned composedly. "Go ahead, and no tricks. I can handle this thing myself if necessary, so I don't really need you."

The engineer understood the significance of the remark. He ground his teeth and moved the engine ahead. It rolled past the switchstand and the shivering brakeman, who caught the grab-irons and climbed into the cab at the mounted man's order. The other gunman moved back against the coal gate chains so he could keep all three train-men covered. The exhaust purred, the great drivers turned over smoothly and the engine moved on up the tracks toward a rather sharp curve that swung through tall brush that obscured the tracks ahead. The mounted man kept pace with the slowly traveling locomotive, leading his companion's horse.

Faint with distance came a mellow whistle note. "There she comes!" chattered the engineer. "She's blowing for the Cibola crossing, less'n two miles ahead."

"Keep this thing moving," said the gunman.

The pony wheels screeched on the curve, the locomotive lurched as it took the turn. Another moment and the straight-away came into view. Far ahead was what looked like a long worm traveling toward them at a prodigious pace.

"All right!" barked the gunman. "Unload! Leave the throttle cracked."

The trainmen obeyed, dropping to the ground one after another and rushing away from the track till the mounted man halted them. At the same instant half a dozen more horsemen, all masked, streamed from the nearby brush. Foremost was a very tall, broad-shouldered man mounted on a sorrel horse. A bristle of short black whiskers showed below his mask. The group, and the other two, paced the slowly moving locomotive.

The Sunrise Limited was late and making up time. Bouncing around on his seatbox, old Pat Bishop, the fat and jolly engineer, expertly jockeyed throttle and reverse bar, getting the last modicum of speed from the great locomotive. Stack purring, siderods flashing a clanking blur, a squirrel-tail of steam floating back from her safety valve, the big engine crashed over the rails. The long train flashed like a meteor past thicket and grove and rolling rangeland.

The engine lurched and swayed around a curve. The fireman let out a warning yell —

"Look out, Pat! There's some damn fool coming this way! Look out!"

Old Pat slammed the throttle shut, grabbed the air valve lever and "wiped the gauge." Air screamed through the port. The brake shoes ground against the wheels. The safety valve lifted with a shattering roar. Black smoke swirled and eddied.

"Why the heck don't he stop?" howled the fireman, leaping from his seatbox and dropping down the steps to stand on the bottom one, hanging onto the grab irons and peering ahead with bulging eyes.

Over went the reverse bar. Bishop jerked the throttle wide open. The stack boomed and bellowed, clots of fire shooting up through the boiling smoke and steam. The great drivers, working in reverse, planed long shavings of steel from the rails. The locomotive leaped and bucked like an outlaw horse. Air screamed through the port as the brake shoes once more clanged against the wheels, and held. And the approaching locomotive kept on its slow but inexorable progress.

With throttle, brakes and reverse bar, old Pat fought to save his train; but to no avail. The two locomotives met head-on with a thunderous crash. The freight engine was knocked clean from the rails to lie on its back beside the right-of-way. The passenger locomotive slewed sideways, rocked, swayed and turned over on its side, steam screeching from broken pipes. The express car of the Limited also left the rails and hung crazily with its rear trucks jammed against the ties. Old Pat, screaming with pain, was pinned beneath the crumpled side of the cab and the hot boilerhead.

The group of masked men surged forward. Shots cracked as bullets were sprayed along the side of the train. From the jammed coaches came the cries of injured and frightened passengers.

Something, hissing and sputtering, sailed through the air, struck the express car door with a thunderous explosion. The door flew to pieces. Three of the outlaws dismounted and ran toward the car. They clambered in. Two shots sounded inside the car, then silence. The tall man sat his sorrel horse a little to one side, directing operations.

Inside the baggage car sounded a muffled boom. A few minutes later the three owl-hoots reappeared, carrying plumped-out canvas bags. The group mounted. A last volley of shots was fired along the train. The outlaws wheeled their horses and galloped into the brush.

It was all over in ten minutes. The robbers rode off with fifty thousand dollars in specie, leaving behind them a wrecked train, a badly injured engineer and a dead express messenger.

Nearly two hours passed before a wreck train and a sheriff's posse arrived. The sheriff trailed the outlaw band to the Rio Grande, beyond which lay the purple mountains of Mexico and safety. In angry disgust, the posse rode back to Cibola.

The Page papers did not procrastinate.
JIM HATFIELD STRIKES AGAIN

11.

Deep in the Chisos foothills, Jim Hatfield bent over a frying pan that crackled and sputtered on a bed of coals. In the pan, a pair of grouse breasts were browning nicely. On another bed of coals steamed a bucket of coffee. Hatfield whistled tunefully as he turned the breasts with a fork. On all sides of the little clearing in which his fire was built, the growth was dense.

Suddenly the fork poised motionless for an instant. Then he laid it across the handle of the pan, still whistling. In a single cat-like bound, he was beyond the circle of firelight, a cocked gun in each hand.

"Come out!" he called harshly. "Come out of it, before I blast you out!"

There was a rustling in the growth and a tall man stepped into view, his white teeth showing in a grin.

"Senor," he said, "Is it your custom to greet an *amigo* with bullets?"

Hatfield uncocked and holstered his guns. "Pancho Arango!" he exclaimed. "Where did *you* come from?"

Arango gestured widely with a dark hand. "From here, there, and everywhere," he replied lightly. "You are a hard one to track down, *Capitan* — I prefer to call you so. But, *Capitan,* I hunger."

"Good!" Hatfield answered. "I'll throw in a couple more hunks of grouse."

Arango shrugged a pack from his shoulders. "And, with other things, I have here the meat of *El Venado* — the deer," he announced. "Ha! we shall feast indeed."

He dived into the pack and brought forth a number of packages, one neatly wrapped. He removed the wrappings with great care and displayed a most delectable looking fruit cake.

"*She* sent you this, *Capitan.* With her own hands she baked it."

"She?"

"*Si. La Senorita* with hair like a forest pool brimful of sunset."

"Well, I'll be!" Hatfield muttered.

"I also have the tortillas, freshly baked, and the small bottle of tequila. So first we will make merry."

"Fine!" chuckled Hatfield, busying himself over the skillet. "Pull up a chair!"

Young Arango rolled a convenient boulder into place, sat down and began manufacturing a *cigarrillo.*

"I have much to tell you, *Capitan,*" he said, "but first the message from her."

"Yes?" Hatfield looked up from the skillet.

"*Si.* She wishes to see you, *Capitan,* and so does the *patrono, Don Tomaso.*"

"You mean Weston?"

"That is right. He requests that you come to visit him, as his guest. But *La Senorita* wishes to see you first. It was she who sent me to find you."

"Then they don't believe that —"

"The *senoritas* are not easily fooled, *Capitan,* especially where a man is concerned, and *Don Tomaso* is far from being loco, except over matters of conquest."

"Well, I'm glad to hear that," Hatfield said. "I'd hate to have either one of them think badly of me."

"Be assured, *Capitan,* they both think most well."

"Let's eat," Hatfield suggested.

They ate, washing down the appetizing meals with draughts of steaming coffee. Then both lighted cigarettes and relaxed in full-fed comfort.

Pancho proceeded to give Hatfield a graphic account of the robbery of the Sunrise Limited and the newspaper comments on the outrage.

"So that's his game," Hatfield mused. "Of course the tall jigger on a sorrel horse was Pedro Cartina."

"Without a doubt, *Capitan,*" Pancho agreed. "It will give me the great pleasure to peg that *ladrone* atop an anthill in the sun, smeared with honey and with his eyelids cut off."

"You don't have much faith in him any more, then?"

"*Capitan,* I have not. For a while I dreamed a dream, that he was the one who was promised, who would bring freedom and happiness to my oppressed people; but it seems I shall have to look elsewhere."

They talked for a while of inconsequential things. Hatfield was, meanwhile, thinking deeply. His problem was becoming more complicated, but in the seemingly mounting difficulty, he began to see opportunity.

Pancho had removed his sombrero and was leaning back against the boulder, the firelight throwing his hawk face in stern relief. Hatfield noticed what he had overlooked before, that the thatch of hair upon his finely shaped head was not black as he had first thought, but rufous, and that his eyes were almost topaz in color.

"Yes," he remarked aloud, "your hair has

a distinct cast of red, Pancho. Wonder how come?"

The young Mexican shrugged. "Doubtless from some far-off ancestor who was not an *Indio*," he replied.

Hatfield thought it likely. Some stray clot of conquistador, some untraceable strain of Celtiberian blood, perhaps. And it had also bequeathed thick shoulders and a gorilla-like chest uncommon to the sinewy Indian or even the pure Castilian-Spaniard. He studied Pancho with interest. He was not an ordinary type. There was power, perhaps unrealized as yet, but potential in his darkly handsome face, and intelligence in the steady eyes. A thought suddenly struck him.

"That night when I first met you, at Kepnau's village, you told me your name was Doroteo Arango, but that you were mostly called Pancho. How come? I can't see any derivative of Pancho from Doroteo."

The Mexican boy laughed a little, whimsically. "My great-uncle," he explained, "was Francisco Villa. They called him the great outlaw of Oaxaca, — the *haciendados* by whom he was hated and feared. He fought for the peons and the other oppressed of my people. A great name! Pancho, as you doubtless know, is a familiar form of Francisco. He has been dead for thirty years and more, but old men who knew him say I resemble him greatly in appearance. So they took to calling me Pancho. I like the name."

"So do I," Hatfield nodded. "A fine sounding name — Pancho Villa. *Veeya! Veeya!* Sounds like the scream of the mountain lion. Perhaps you should take all of it instead of just half."

Pancho laughed again. "Perhaps I will, some day," he said, "but it is — what you say — presumption to borrow the name of a great one, is it not?"

"Not if you live up to it," Hatfield instantly countered.

"Perhaps," Pancho repeated. "*Mi amigo, visiones grandes son pintodas en mi corazon* — My friend, great visions are painted on my heart!"

He sat brooding into the fire, and watching him, Hatfield was convinced that the day would come when he would indeed add lustre to the name.

Hatfield could not, of course, look into the future and see the countless thousands marching to the strains of *La Cucaracha* behind a man with topaz eyes who by his deeds of reckless daring, before he died in a blood-bath, would lay the foundations of a free Mexico. Pancho Villa! A bugle call to the peons of *Mejico!* The Wild Heart that did not beat in vain!

12.

"Capitan," Pancho said, "I have more to tell you. I rode through the River villages before I came to you and listened to men talk. Many there are of Cartina's men and they know his plans. He intends to strike again, and soon."

"Looks like Page has given him a free hand," Hatfield mused. "He's always held him in leash this side of the River, to a certain extent."

"Yes," agreed Pancho, "but those days are done. Masquerading as yourself, the more frequent his depredations, the better the *Senor* Page will be pleased."

"Looks like it's up to me to tangle Cartina's twine for him, if possible," Hatfield observed.

"Us," Pancho corrected. "From now on I ride with you, *Capitan;* only soon we must ride to *la hacienda de Don Tomaso.* I promised *La Senorita* that you would."

"Okay," Hatfield agreed, "but have you any notion what Cartina is up to?"

"The whispers are many," said Pancho, "but I think I have winnowed the truth from the chaff."

Pancho talked, while Hatfield smoked and listened, interjecting a question now and then. After the Mexican had finished and paused, expectant, Hatfield sat silent for several minutes.

"I believe we can work it," he said slowly at length. "If what you learned turns out to be straight talk, I think we may be able to tangle Cartina's twine for him in a way he won't soon forget, if he lives to remember."

"Capitan," Pancho replied, "I am confident what I told you is true. And I believe, too, that it is opportunity for us. But one favor I would ask — leave Cartina for me. I have scores to settle with that *ladrone.*"

"Okay," Hatfield agreed, albeit a bit reluctantly, "but don't forget you are going up against a hard man. There is no fear in Pedro Cartina. He never takes a chance that isn't necessary. He thinks always of himself and lays his plans accordingly. He has a cool, calculating brain and an utterly ruthless nature. He is for Pedro Cartina, first, last, and all the time. He'll throw anybody to the wolves if it will be to his personal advantage to do so. Just as he had you stand in the firelight that night in Kepnau's village. Cartina didn't do that because he was afraid. I don't think he knows what fear is. But because it was to his advantage for you

116

to take a chance slug or have something happen to you instead of him, just as it worked out that night. Don't underestimate him. He's the sort you can't give a break. Give him one and he'll take 'em all. Don't forget."

After which they built up the fire, spread their blankets beside it and went to sleep.

They were up with the dawn and after breakfast Hatfield got busy.

"Got to make a few preparations," he told his companion. "If I go barging into town as I am now, we'll be leading a posse out. Which won't help us and will help Cartina."

For an hour and more he browsed about amid the thickets, digging out a root here, collecting a handful of leaves there, and a few clusters of berries. He returned to the camp, laid out his loot and set a bucket of water on the fire. When it came to a boil, he added portions of the roots, berries and leaves, taking great care as to the proportion of each. He let the mixture boil for half an hour, then set it aside to cool. When the solids had settled to the bottom, he had a clear, pale liquid almost as colorless as water but with a peculiar glassy look to it. As Pancho watched with intense interest, Hatfield, with the aid of a tiny mirror applied the mixture to his hair with great nicety. Also to the already respectable stubble of black beard that had sprouted on cheeks and chin.

"Madre de Dios!" marvelled Pancho when the operation was complete. "*Capitan,* you look twenty years older. Your hair it is gray and your beard also. It is the miracle!"

"Hardly that," Hatfield chuckled. "An old Karanakawa Indian down around Matagorda Bay taught me how to brew the compound. The Kranks were the poison people of the Indians, you know, and there wasn't much about herbs and things they didn't know. It's come in handy before. Water won't touch it, but plenty of soap will take it out. Nope, you don't need any. Nobody knows you and won't pay any attention to you. After a little work on Goldy I figure we ought to get by."

The great sorrel watched the operation with suspicion but did not protest. Nor did he seem perturbed that, after Hatfield finished with his glossy hide and the mixture, he had become a pretty fair imitation of a *bayo* skew-bald. He merely snorted and went back to cropping grass.

"Now we'd better be moving," Hatfield said. "We've got a pretty good ride ahead of us and we don't want to push our horses. We may need all they've got to give before the day is over."

The night before, Pancho had led a big powerful looking bay into the clearing. Now he proceeded to get the rig on him while Hatfield packed the cooking utensils. Five minutes later they rode down the brush-covered slope together.

"By the way," Hatfield asked, "how'd you find me last night?"

Pancho smiled. "A word here, a whisper there," he replied. "You were seen from time to time by those who bear you no enmity. To others their lips were sealed, but to me they spoke freely. I guessed you would make for the Chisos country — all hunted men do — and beside here would be close to Cartina's hunting ground. So yesterday evening, as the dusk fell, I watched the sky. I saw the faint stain of smoke against the sky. The rest was easy. *Indio* eyes are sharp, *Capitan*."

Hatfield agreed. "I built that little fire of dry wood, and it was already getting dark."

"But the sky was still bright, as was the upper air," Pancho replied. "Something to remember, *Capitan*."

"You're right there," Hatfield admitted, "but I don't think the eyes of a white man could have noticed it."

"Well, here we go," he added a moment later as the brush began to thin. "Hope we

119

don't meet many folks on the way. Others besides *Indios* have sharp eyes at times. Don't want to get into a shindig, especially with somebody I've no desire to trade lead with. Well-meaning gents can sometimes be a nuisance. Don't forget what I told you about Cartina. Don't underestimate him or you're liable to be sorry. He's a salty hombre, and he's got plenty of wrinkles on his horns."

13.

Northward from the awful gorge that bounds the Texas Big Bend country on the south, a trail slithers like a crippled snake past the blue mystery of the Chisos Mountains. It was an old trail when the Spaniard first set foot on Texas soil; old when the Aztecs followed it south in quest of empire; old when the first moccasin padded over it; old, doubtless, when beetle-browned, crooked boned men with low, curving skulls slunk along it, glancing fearfully into the depths of the rank growth that festered under a red sun. For it is the trail to the gateway of the north.

Over parched desert and arid flat it winds. Through canyon and gorge, in the shadow of towering mountain walls; along the verge of dizzy precipices, it makes its way. Over it sway great clusters of the lily-white blossoms that give it its name — the *yuccas,* ghost flowers of the desert, thriving amid desolation and death.

But finally the Yucca trail leaves the wastelands for a while and runs through a veritable garden spot that centers around Talley Mountain, locally called Cow Heaven.

All morning and till well past noon, Hatfield and Pancho rode the Yucca trail, meeting only a few stray cowhands and a wandering prospector or two. They rode steadily but easily, heading for the town of Marta in the shadow of Talley Mountain.

Marta might be likened to the hub of a wheel, the perimeter of which was the rich rangeland on all sides. The spokes were the trails leading to the gold and quicksilver mines in the hills. Marta was the focal point for a region as large as some eastern states. Its great general stores were stocked with all that was needful to cowhand and miner. Its bank was usually heavily stocked with money to take care of payrolls and mine and ranch expenses. Deposits of gold were also frequent and large.

Marta's locus was strategic in that the broad Yucca trail ran directly north to the railroad, easy traveling by stages and wagons, which kept supplies flowing freely between the town and the country. Marta was a peaceful and rather sleepy town, except on paydays when the cowhands raised hell. Due to its isolation, Marta was not pestered much by outlaw bands. Even minor depredations were infrequent. But its very complacency, Hatfield knew, made the town vulnerable to a daring and well-planned raid. Towns nearer the Border were prepared for such eventualities and their citizens were normally on the *qui vive.* But Marta drowsed in the shadow of its mountain.

Things were certainly quiet enough when Hatfield and Pancho rode into the town. The citizens were going about their business in a leisurely manner. A few horses stood at the racks with half-closed eyes and hanging heads and drooping ears. Dogs scratched industriously in the shade. Roosters scratched just as industriously in the sun, striving to unearth provender for clucking and expectant hens. The bank building looked solid and substantial. A saloon diagonally opposite looked cool and inviting.

Hatfield and Pancho hitched their horses loosely at a nearby rack and entered the saloon. The place was quiet. A couple of desert rats drank silently at the far end of the bar. Several townspeople sat at a table. A jovial bartender approached and asked them to name their "pizen."

Hatfield had chosen a position not far from the door. Through a window he had a clear view of the front door of the bank. He had already noticed that the building sat on the outskirts of the town. The street which ran past it was the continuation of a trail that curved around a grove not fifty yards distant.

The travelers sipped their drinks. Nobody paid any attention to them after a casual glance. The saloon was pleasantly dusky after the glare of the sun outside. The whole town seemed half-asleep; only the roosters in the dust created movement in the street.

And then abruptly the peace irrupted into explosive action. Around the bend raced eight mounted men, hat-brims drawn low, neckerchiefs muffled about their chins. The foremost, forking a fine sorrel horse boasted the added concealment of a *serape* draped across his shoulder.

"It's them!" Hatfield exclaimed, and bounded for the door.

The outlaws worked with the precision of a machine. Two of their number flung from the saddles and raced into the bank. There came the sound of a shot and a cry of pain. Startled citizens stuck heads out of doors and jerked them back as bullets sprayed the buildings.

When Hatfield and Pancho reached the street, two more of the outlaws were in the act of dismounting. Hatfield's big Colts bucked in his hands. Their muzzles streamed fire and smoke. He emptied two saddles with two shots and downed a third man who ran from the bank, a smoking gun in his hand. The horses reared and squealed, the owlhoots fired wildly in return. Slugs stormed past or kicked up puffs of dust. Hatfield continued to fire.

Pancho ran forward and was taking deliberate aim at the tall man on the sorrel horse. But the other hurled himself sideways in a flash of movement, one sinewy leg hooked around the saddle horn, assuming the position favored by the Plains Indians when circling an embattled wagon train. He fired under his horse's neck.

Pancho's hat flew from his head. He reeled back, blood streaming down his face. Blinded by the blood in his eyes he emptied his gun futilely. Hatfield tried to line sights with the tall leader, but a horse plunged in front of the other and spoiled his aim. The rider of the sorrel whirled his mount and went streaking back the way he had come, his surviving followers thundering after him. A man reeled in his saddle but kept to the hull as Hatfield fired his last cartridge.

"Come on!" the Lone Wolf shouted, running for his horse. Pancho wavered and stumbled after him, seemingly on the verge of falling, but managed to mount the bay. Together they tore past the bank in the wake of the fleeing owlhoots.

As they passed, Hatfield leaned over and glanced into the faces of three dead men sprawled in the dust.

"Parker, Haynes and Tally!" he muttered. "Three of those skunks, all right, and the owlhoot in the blanket was Cartina."

With Goldy slightly in the lead, they careened around the bend and vanished from sight of the town.

Meanwhile all was confusion and uproar in Marta. A man came staggering from the bank, clutching a reddened shirt sleeve.

"Did you see him?" he yelled. "By God, that was Jim Hatfield!"

"You mean the big feller on the sorrel?" somebody shouted back. "Why — that —"

"Sorrel, *hell!*" bawled the wounded cashier. "I mean the feller who rode off on the spotted horse, the feller who downed those three murdering buzzards!"

"Hell, that feller's hair and whiskers were gray — he was years older'n Hatfield," somebody protested. "Besides, they say Hatfield has tied up with an owlhoot outfit himself."

"And I'm telling you and telling the world that whoever says that is loco!" stormed the cashier, wringing his bloodstained hands. "Owlhoots don't bust up robberies and shoot the robbers. I tell you it was Hatfield. I saw him in action once before, and if you see him once, you don't forget him. And he was fighting on the side of law and order, per usual. Owlhoot, hell! Don't make me laugh! I ain't in no mood for laughing! Somebody give me a rag to tie up this arm, and fetch the doctor. I don't feel so good."

14.

When Hatfield and Pancho rounded the bend, the fleeing outlaws were far in advance, and very quickly Hatfield saw it was no use. Pancho was reeling in his saddle and unable to handle the reins properly. His horse stumbled, recovered, stumbled again. Hatfield reined Goldy back, seized the bay's bit iron and turned the heads of both horses into the thin straggle of brush that edged the trail.

"It's no go," he told Pancho. "You may be hurt worse than you think. Got to get you someplace where I can look you over and give you attention. Hang onto the horn, I'll handle the horse."

He looped the reins over his arms as he spoke and rode on, the bay trotting beside Goldy. For some distance he diagonalled through the brush, working steadily away from the trail.

Pancho was recovering somewhat. He had let go the horn and was sitting erect, swearing in two languages.

"Told you you'd be up against a smart and salty hombre," Hatfield reminded him. "That hellion doesn't miss a bet. You're lucky he didn't drill you dead center. Guess the very fact he is so smart is what saved you. He'd figured the whole angle in a split second. If he'd taken time for another shot, the chances are I'd have gotten him. He knew it and didn't take the chance. Swerved his horse so the rest of the buzzards would be between me and him, and away he went. Well, we did for three of them, anyhow, and I think I burned that second one coming out of the bank rather hard. He was swaying as he rode away, and I've a notion this gave Cartina considerable of a jolt. Guess the last thing he expected was us to show up like we did. If we can just get him jumpy enough, he's liable to make a bad slip and give us our real chance. Same goes for Page. He won't feel so good over what happened when he hears about it. Wonder what he'll be able to make of it? He'll make something, all right."

"Give me the reins," Pancho said. "I can handle them now. And that *ladrone* escaped me! *Cien mil diablos!* He moves like the flash of the lightning!"

"He may not be a hundred thousand devils, but he's sure a good imitation of one," Hatfield replied. "Well, better luck next time. Wonder what's going on in the town back there? Got a notion they're a bunch of puzzled gents about now."

A little later they reached a ravine that wound into the hills in an easterly direction. Soon it became a very respectable canyon with steeply sloping walls which grew wilder and more rugged as they progressed.

"Another hour and we should be well in the clear," Hatfield decided. "We'll keep going until it begins to get dark. No telling what's going on back in town and I don't want to tangle with a posse. They might take the wrong trail when they light out after those varmints. And we don't want to have to do any explaining. Better to keep 'em guessing for a while."

"The next time there will be no guessing for some people," Pancho fumed. "Not again will I miss."

"You should learn to shoot without raising your gun," Hatfield told him. "You need considerable practice on the draw. I'll have to take you in hand, I guess. And something to keep in mind, it isn't the first shot fired that counts, it's the first shot that reaches the mark. Better to take a mite of time and let the other fellow waste lead. If he's in too much of a hurry, there's a good chance he'll miss, and before he steadies his hand you can get in the one that means something. Let him have one on the house, but never two."

Pancho nodded, and there was a gleam of purpose in his eye. In that moment lay the beginnings of the career of one of the finest shots the Western hemisphere ever knew.

"Things happened fast back there," he remarked. "Everything in but the few seconds."

"Uh-huh, it was a right lively corpse-and-cartridge session while it lasted," Hatfield agreed. "Well, here looks to be a likely spot for camp. Good overhang and a spring, and plenty of dry wood in sight. I could stand a helping right now and a few cups of hot coffee. Long time since we ate."

First of all, Hatfield examined Pancho's wounded head. "You just lost a bit of hair and some skin," he announced. "But even a grazing slug hits hard. A little to the left and you'd be back there with those others. That buzzard sure can handle a gun."

Anton Page was able to turn the abortive hold-up to his own advantage. A scarehead article proclaimed that Jim Hatfield and his gang had attempted to rob the Marta Bank — the names and identities of the three dead men were disclosed — and had been thwarted by two unknown cowhands. That the cowhands had not come forward to claim the approbation due them was not strange, said the article. Doubtless they preferred to keep their identity concealed for fear of vengeance that might be wreaked upon them by the renegade Ranger, or, the article broadly hinted, by other Rangers who would resent their interference.

But the cashier of the Marta Bank was a thoroughly aroused man. In addition to being cashier, he was one of the bank's largest stockholders, a ranchowner and a holder of valuable mining shares. His fellow-townsmen were wont to give an ear to his opinions and he had influential connections in other parts of the state. He sent storming telegrams to Captain Bill McDowell, the Adjutant General and the Governor. And to associates in positions of authority. Before he knew it, Anton Page found himself involved in a raging controversy. And, an unique experience for him, also found himself for once on the defensive and called upon to explain.

Not for a moment however did he ease his vigorous campaign against the Rangers in general and Jim Hatfield in particular; but he was bombarded with questions that proved difficult to answer. More definite proof of his allegations was demanded from many quarters and a rival sheet went so far as to hint that Page might not be altogether motivated by an altruistic desire for cleaner government and stricter law enforcement.

Page proceeded to blast the offender off the face of the earth — in print. But the editor in question was a vigorous and coura- geous young man and refused to be blasted. His reply to the Page fulmination was brief and to the point. He demanded facts, not bluster.

All of which indicated uncertainty and confusion in the camp of the enemy.

■ ■ ■ ■

Pancho's wound proved more serious than at first thought. The following morning he was running a high fever and complained of violent pains in his head. His face was flushed, his pulse accelerated.

Hatfield browsed the thickets for herbs and berries from which he concocted a healing poultice and a draft to bring down his temperature. Another twenty-four hours and he was seriously contemplating taking a chance and summoning a doctor from Marta. But Pancho insisted that he wait awhile. Hatfield reluctantly agreed.

For three days the Mexican youth's condition was far from satisfactory, but on the fourth night the fever broke and the next day found him normal though weak. Two more days elapsed, however, before he got his strength back sufficiently to be up and about.

"And now, *Capitan,*" he insisted, "we must ride north. I promised *her,* and a promise unkept is a debt unpaid."

"Wonder why she's so anxious to see me?" Hatfield said.

Pancho smiled a little. "I think the answer is obvious," he remarked.

"Why the devil!" Hatfield snorted. "She only saw me once, for a minute."

Pancho smiled again. "The ways of the *senoritas* are most mysterious," he replied. "But aside from *that,*" assuming a graver tone, "I think she has something important to tell you. I could gather so much from her manner. Remember, she hears and sees much in *el loco hacienda.* Many men of many kinds visit there and talk with the *pa-trono.* There is the much brains under the flame-colored hair of that small head. *She* sees what Don Tomaso, bemused by his dreams, does not. But be that as it may, she commands and we must obey."

"All right," Hatfield chuckled, "but my experience has been that wherever women get mixed up in things, trouble follows."

"Agreed," said Pancho. "All too often they are death to a man — but what a way to die!"

15.

They broke camp at dusk and headed north, riding slowly and warily, following little used trails that brought them to within a couple of miles of Weston's Running W ranchhouse. While it was still dark they holed up in a dense thicket, kindled a small fire of dry wood and cooked something to eat. Then they lay down and slept till well past noon. A few hours later Pancho got the rig on his big bay.

"I will ride alone to the *hacienda,*" he said. "It is best that way. No telling who may be around. I will seek out *La Senorita* and talk with her. No one will think anything of my absence, for she promised to take care of that."

Hatfield thought the plan good and offered no objection. He didn't care to run the chance of barging into the sheriff of the county, who he knew often visited Weston. After Pancho left, he smoked and took it easy, wondering just what information the Mexican might gather. It was not far from dark when he heard the clicking of a horse's irons coming toward the thicket Very quickly he realized that two animals were drawing near. In the shadow of the deeper brush he waited.

Pancho's big bay pushed his nose through the growth. Following him came a splendid blue moros that carried Sylvia Mayfield.

Hatfield stepped forward and removed his hat. The redheaded girl stared at him, then burst into a giggle.

"All you need is black velvet, silver *conchas,* and a *serape* and you'd be perfect," she declared. "One of the stately *hidalgos* of Mexico! Really, the gray hair and beard become you. Most distinguished looking!"

"Now you see how I'll look twenty years from now," Hatfield said, falling in with her mood.

"Then you have nothing to worry about," she returned lightly. "Then you'll look mature, and not so boyish as you did the last time I saw you."

"Boyish! I'm past thirty!"

"So young? Well, I suppose you can't help that, but time will take care of it for you."

"I don't see how you have much room to talk," he grumbled. "You can't be more than twenty-five yourself!"

"I'm just past twenty!" she returned, rather hastily. "Oh, all right, I fell for that one! I'll get even with you, see if I don't. But I've something more serious to talk about right now."

She swung her leg over the saddle, but Hatfield reached up, circled her tiny waist with his hands and lifted her lightly to the ground. For a moment he held her, cradled close, and she showed no disposition to be free. She blushed prettily when he dropped her on her feet, and shot him a quick look from her long-lashed eyes. Pancho smiled in a pleased manner.

Instantly she was grave again, however. "Yes, I have something to talk about that is very important," she said. "A few nights ago my uncle had a visitor."

"Yes?" Hatfield prompted.

"Yes. A man who has been there before, whom my deluded uncle thinks is a great patriot and an ally in his crazy plan — Pedro Cartina."

Hatfield stared at her. Pancho muttered under his breath.

"Pedro Cartina," she repeated. "For a while they talked of my uncle's schemes. Cartina assured him that the Indian tribes on both sides of the Rio Grande were ready to follow his banner when he marched into Mexico. Then somehow, I am pretty sure Cartina steered the conversation — I didn't hear everything that was said — the talk got around to you. My uncle said he did not believe what was said of you. Cartina instantly agreed with him. Cartina said that Anton Page was sincere in his beliefs, but mistaken, that he had told him so and tried to persuade him to stop his newspaper campaign against you. That pleased my uncle."

Hatfield and Pancho looked at each other. They waited expectantly for what else was to come.

"Cartina asked my uncle, quite casually, if he had seen you lately. My uncle told him that you had been to the ranchhouse only once, when you were brought there, but that he hoped to see you again, that he had sent word to you that he wanted to talk to you."

"And what did Cartina say to that?" Hatfield asked.

"He told my uncle he thought it a splendid idea, and asked when he expected to see you, again very casually. My uncle said he did not know for sure but hoped and expected that it would be soon. Cartina looked very pleased. Does that mean anything to you?"

"Considerable," Hatfield replied grimly. "Anything else?"

"Nothing except generalities concerning the march to Mexico. But I was frightened by the expression in Cartina's eyes. They're terrible eyes. I hate them. They — *look* at me!"

Hatfield's lips tightened. Pancho said something in Spanish that would not bear translating. But Hatfield, seeing that she was really frightened, tried to carry the matter off lightly.

"Can't blame him overmuch for looking," he replied. "I sort of looked myself the other night when you were wearing that very pretty robe."

"*He* never saw me in that," she replied with asperity. "And there are looks, and *looks*." The dimple showed at the corner of her mouth. "And who does the looking means something, too," she added.

"I think," Pancho said, "that I will go and see if someone comes," and he slipped silently into the growth.

"Pancho presumes, I'm afraid," Hatfield said with a smile.

Again the dimple showed. "Well," she said, "I didn't tell him to go, did I? Perhaps — oh!" A little later. "But I really have to breathe — a little."

Pancho took his time about coming back, but he was not particularly missed.

"Oh, by the way," Sylvia exclaimed, "I heard something else you might think important. On the night of the new moon — that's the ninth, isn't it? — Cartina and some of the tribal chiefs are to meet with Anton Page at Page's ranchhouse."

Hatfield looked thoughtful. "And today's the second," he remarked. "Sounds interesting."

"Are you going to see my uncle tonight?" Sylvia asked.

Hatfield shook his head, "I had intended to, but after what you told me about Cartina, I don't think it advisable. At least, not right away."

The girl's quick mind caught the meaning of his remark. Her eyes widened.

"You — you mean you think Cartina might lay a trap for you?"

"Wouldn't be at all surprised," Hatfield replied. "In fact, I think it very probable, from the way he wormed it out of your uncle that he expected me to come to see him soon. It's made to order for Cartina. All he'd need to do is keep tabs on the ranchhouse."

Sylvia looked frightened. "Perhaps he knows you are here now," she said.

"Oh, I reckon not," Hatfield answered lightly. "But honey, I think you'd better be getting back to the house. Pancho will ride with you."

"I'll be all right myself," she said.

"Chances are, but I'd rather you didn't ride alone," he replied. "Be dark before you get there. I'll be seeing you."

"Soon?"

"I hope."

He caught her up in his arms for a moment and held her close. "Guess it finally happens to everybody," he chuckled.

"*Si!* Even to *El Lobo Solo*," said Pancho.

"He's been a Lone Wolf long enough," she

declared energetically. "Take care of yourself, dear."

He lifted her lightly to the saddle. "Be seeing you," he said.

Engrossed in saying good-bye, she did not note the swift glance that passed between Hatfield and Pancho. The young Mexican nodded his head almost imperceptibly, and surreptitiously loosened his guns in their sheaths.

As soon as they had passed from sight, Hatfield moved into the deeper shadow, first slipping his heavy Winchester from the saddle boot. He placed Goldy within hand's reach and dropped the split reins to the ground as a sign he must not move.

"May be nothing to it," he told the sorrel, "but Cartina's riders have sharp eyes and are good at figuring things out. They may have tied up her ride down here with Pancho. If they have, things might get interesting when he heads back this way. Best not to take chances."

While the twilight faded to dusk and the dusk deepened to dark, he stood silent and motionless, straining his ears for the click of hoofs that would herald Pancho's return; and for stealthy sounds that might be made by someone else.

The night was very still. A soft hush

brooded over the rangeland and not a breath of air stirred. The slow minutes dragged past and Hatfield began to grow acutely uneasy. He estimated that Pancho had had time to make the trip to the ranch-house and back. Of course he might have paused to chat with somebody, but Hatfield thought that unlikely. He would doubtless avoid all contacts at a time when portentous events might be shaping. Hatfield figured he would deliver his charge to the ranch-house and then fade unobtrusively into the darkness. He should have been back before now.

Somewhere to the north an owl hooted, persistently. To the south a coyote yipped, was silent, yipped again. The owl hooted, with a kind of unnatural screaming note. And once more the coyote uttered its querulous half-bark, half-whine. Hatfield's brows drew together. He had a premonition of impending evil.

And then he caught the sound of hoofs clicking out of the north, and clicking fast. He waited, tense and expectant. The drumming beats grew louder. There was a crashing of brush and Pancho rode into view, jerking his mount to a slithering halt.

"*Capitan,* men come from the north," he gasped. "They are still some ways off, but they come fast."

16.

"We played a straight hunch," Hatfield said quietly. "It's a trap. Okay, here we go. No, not to the trail. We'd be settin' ducks. It's still light enough for straight shootin'. Sky is clear as a bell and plenty of stars."

"Surely we can outride them," Pancho protested as Hatfield led the way through the growth, heading east by south.

"Sure," Hatfield agreed, "and right into the arms of the hellions waiting down below. Remember that belt of chaparral that flanks the trail a mile or so to the south? That's where they're holed up. I got their signal. Handled pretty well, but I've heard Indians imitate birds and animals before. They're good, but there's always a little difference if your ears are keen enough to catch it. But we've got to work it smart. I've a notion we're up against Cartina's Yaquis and they've got plenty of savvy. I think we can make it by circling around on the prairie. Grass is very thick down here and should drown out the hoofbeats if we take it slow. But be ready to grab your horse's nose if he takes a notion to sing. Take your neck cloth off and wind it around the bit irons. A jingle carries a long way when it's so quiet. Yes, I figure they'll expect us to take to the trail, where we could make good time. When the bunch to the north don't see us ride out of the thicket, it should puzzle them and slow them up. While they're investigating this brush, we'll be putting distance between us and them. When we get behind that chaparral belt, we'll see. I've a little idea that we may be able to tangle *Senor* Cartina's twine for him again. Worth trying, anyhow. If we slip — well, we won't be around to worry about it, but we'll take a chance."

"If I can just get opportunity to line sights with that *ladrone,* I will take the chance," fumed Pancho as they emerged from the straggle of growth.

"He might be with one of the gangs, but I rather doubt it," Hatfield said. "This is the sort of chore he gives to the hands. I've a notion he underestimates us a mite."

At a fast walk they sent their horses ahead. Hatfield glanced back from time to time to make sure they were keeping in line with the big thicket in which they had holed up. He figured that the bunch from the north would approach the growth with caution and give them the time they needed to get in the clear. The only catch in the procedure was that it was just possible that the shrewd

Yaquis would have taken this very possibility into consideration and would have a guard posted in the rear of the chaparral belt to watch the prairie to the east. If that happened to be the case, Hatfield told Pancho, they wouldn't be around long enough to worry about it.

As they drew away from the thicket, Hatfield began to feel easier on the one score. Now they had little to fear from the pursuit to the north. But with each pace of the horses, the danger ahead assumed greater proportions. It was a far from comfortable feeling, drawing nearer and nearer to the ominous black bristle of chaparral and what it doubtless concealed. Were beady black eyes at the very moment gloatingly watching their approach — eyes that glittered back of rifle sights, the muzzles shifting ever so slightly to keep the moving targets in line? Were sinewy fingers tensing to squeeze the stocks and send the messengers of death whizzing toward their victims? A lively imagination is necessary to success in any line of endeavor, but at times it can be something of a curse. As Hatfield gazed toward the silent brush, it became endowed with stealthy and malevolent movement. The crooked branches of the mesquite were as reaching hands and the occasional glint of starlight on a leaf or a bare branch became the gleam of watching eyes. He knew it wasn't so, but the illusion persisted and did not tend for comfort during the slow ride.

And it seemed to him they were taking an unreasonably long time to reach the growth. If the pursuers from the north were, as he assumed, trigger-sensed Yaquis or even Apaches, it would not take them long to discover the thicket was untenanted. Then they would charge from concealment, knowing the quarry must be somewhere ahead. And that would arouse the silent watchers in the chaparral and signal them to divert their attention from the trail. And he and Pancho would be caught between a deadly crossfire and would be forced to head due east toward the broken ground farther on, and be riding the longer leg of the triangle. And either way they turned would draw them nearer to one of the two converging bands of pursuers. Well, another three minutes would tell the tale.

Hatfield heaved a deep sigh of relief when they melted into the deeper shadow of the chaparral belt without alarm from the north. Now they were in much better position. Undoubtedly their approach had not been noticed. If they could continue undetected and discover where the ambush was holed up, the advantage would be theirs.

But that was the question: Just where were the drygulchers hidden? Hatfield reasoned that they would pick a spot near the middle of the belt; but of that he could not be sure. Walking their horses slowly, they moved along in the shadow of the outer struggle. Finally they pulled to a halt and sat listening.

The minutes dragged past, and nothing happened. There was no hint of movement amid the growth.

Hatfield didn't like it. He felt sure that before long the band from the north, becoming convinced that the quarry had escaped the thicket, would join with the others. He didn't want that to happen. He leaned over and set his mouth close to Pancho's ear.

"I'm going to try something," he whispered. "Got a notion maybe it will work."

He sat erect in the saddle, opened his lips and uttered the harsh, weird cry of a disturbed caracara owl. Twice he repeated the cry, then paused to listen.

For a moment the silence endured. Then, from almost directly ahead came the querulous yipping of a coyote. A slight pause and again the yipping. Hatifield waited a moment, then hooted again, drawing out the note as he had earlier heard it come from the north. A single sharp yip answered.

"They fell for it," he whispered to Pancho. "They think the bunch from up the trail is about to join them. Come on. Go slow till you see them. Then hightail straight for them and give them everything you've got. Straight through them and down the trail. Let's go!"

They moved their horses forward through the growth, peering and listening. They caught a glimpse of the white gleam of the trail beyond the chaparral before solider shadows suddenly disengaged from the gloom ahead.

For another instant the ruse was successful. Then a vagrant gleam of starlight rested on Hatfield's face. There was a startled cry, a storm of exclamations. Hatfield's voice rang out —

"Trail, Goldy! Trail!"

The great sorrel leaped forward, Pancho's bay keeping pace. Both Hatfield's guns let go with a rattling crash. Pancho was also shooting with both hands. The startled cries turned to howls of pain and panic. Straight for the demoralized drygulchers they rode. Another moment and they were in the thick of them, gun barrels flailing right and left.

The boom of shots, the screams of the stricken, the solid crunch of steel on bone and the neighing of the frightened horses blended in a hideous pandemonium of sound.

There were nearly a dozen of the drygulchers, but the two charging horsemen knew exactly what they were doing while Cartina's killers were caught completely off balance. Half of their number were down before they really realized what had happened. Before they could collect their wits and offer anything like an effective defense, Hatfield and Pancho were through their broken ranks, out of the growth and pounding along the trail.

But the affair wasn't over. Behind sounded yells and curses, then a rattle of gunfire. Bullets whistled past, too close for comfort. Twisting in his saddle, Hatfield saw seven or eight horsemen charging down the trail only two hundred yards behind. The band from the north had arrived just a moment too late. But neither Hatfield nor Pancho was sure it *had* arrived too late, after all. They were within easy rifle range and the pursuers were throwing lead as fast as they could pull trigger.

Hatfield let the reins fall on Goldy's neck, jerked his rifle from the saddle boot and twisted around, clamping the stock of the heavy Winchester to his shoulder. His eyes glanced along the sights. The rifle bucked. Fire spurted from the muzzle. A man reeled in his saddle. Another uttered a gasping cry and pitched to the ground. Hatfield lowered the sights and fired again.

A horse fell. Another catapaulted over it, flinging its rider from the hull like a stone from a sling. The others tried to pull up but could not. A third horse lost its footing and the battle had become a wild tangle of cursing men and squealing horses. Hatfield slammed the smoking rifle back into the boot as horsemen streamed from the growth behind.

"Ride!" he shouted to Pancho. "I think I slowed 'em up enough. Sift sand!"

Stirrup to stirrup, bending low in their saddles as lead whistled past, they raced down the star-burned trail, with the pursuers falling steadily behind. Three more minutes and they were around a bend and the babble of the discomfited drygulchers was but a drone in the distance.

Pancho was highly exultant. "Long will they remember us, *Capitan,*" he chortled gleefully. "While they curse and lick their wounds."

"Hope so," Hatfield agreed, "but that devil

is a shrewd hombre. He'll move fast in one way or another. I've got a feeling we're a long ways from finished with him yet. Okay, turn off to the left."

"Where are we going, *Capitan?*"

"To the Running W ranchhouse," Hatfield replied. "We have an appointment there, you know; we can't help it if we're a bit late."

Pancho shook with laughter. "A night of surprises," he said.

They circled wide around the chaparral belt and the thicket where they had holed up earlier and approached the ranchhouse from the east. They reached the grove that surrounded it and walked their horses slowly. As Hatfield expected, before they were close to the building, a voice challenged them, backing it up with the click of a rifle hammer drawing back to full cock. They reined instantly. Pancho called out —

"It is I, Pancho Arango. I bring an *amigo* the *patrono* wishes to see."

A moment of silence followed, while the guard took stock. Then he stepped into view, rifle at the ready, peering with outthrust neck.

"Okay, Pancho," he said. "Where you been keeping yourself? Go ahead, the Boss is still up. I'll send the word along and there'll be somebody to take your horses." He whistled a peculiar note, which was instantly answered from a spot nearer the house. Hatfield and Pancho rode forward.

A wrangler was waiting at the steps. Hatfield said a word to Goldy as he dismounted. The wrangler led him and the bay to the stable. Hatfield and Pancho mounted the steps. Evidently they were expected, for the door swung open before they knocked. They stepped into the living room with the big fireplace, where Hatfield had once been held prisoner.

Old Tom Weston was seated by the fire. He rose as they entered.

"Come in, Lieutenant, come in, Pancho," he invited cordially. "Take a load off your feet. Well, Lieutenant, we meet again."

He shook hands with Hatfield and motioned them to chairs.

"Glad to see you both," he said. "Lieutenant, you appear to have aged considerably since last we met. I think gray hair and a beard becomes you. But you don't need to rush them — they'll get there soon enough, as I have reason to know." He ran his fingers through his crinkly white mane as he spoke.

"Figured a little friendly talk was in order," he said. "If you don't mind, I'd like to have my niece present. I think you have already met her, Lieutenant. I rather believe she was the, er — *key* to the situation last time." He chuckled mirthfully and raised his voice —

"Rosa!"

An elderly Mexican woman appeared from an inner door. Her face was as expressionless as a deal board but her eyes were bright and quick.

"Rosa, tell *La Senorita* I want her," Weston said.

"*La Senorita* no here," Rosa replied laconically.

"Not here!"

"No. Man come, give her note. She read note. Ride off together."

"Man! What man?"

"Tall man with scar face. You hire two, three weeks ago."

"Oh, Bert Calloway," Weston replied. "He's all right. Anton Page recommended him to me. But why the devil did she go gallivanting off at this time of night. Women! You can never tell what they're up to. Well, tell her I want her as soon as she gets back."

While he listened to the conversation, Hatfield's face became tense, but his voice was quiet when he spoke. He addressed the Mexican woman in a tone that immediately centered her attention.

"Rosa," he asked, "were any names mentioned?"

" 'Jeem Hatfield', say man with scar," replied Rosa, who evidently did not believe in waste of words.

"What the devil!" exploded old Tom, in bewilderment.

Hatfield turned to him. "I'm afraid this is serious, sir," he said. "I see Pedro Cartina's hand in it. Evidently the note was supposed to be from me."

"But what in hell does it mean?" demanded Weston.

"I'm afraid it means Cartina has abducted Sylvia," Hatfield replied, his voice suddenly like steel grinding on ice. "And he planned to put the blame on me. If things had worked out as he planned, it would have sure looked that way. With me dead and my body done away with. He'd have a dozen men to swear they saw us together. Listen —"

In a few terse sentences he told Weston of the attempted drygulching. When he finished, old Tom rose to his feet, towering over even Hatfield. In his eyes gleamed a maniacal ferocity.

"I'll rouse the whole Border!" he stormed. "I'll have a thousand men on that sidewinder's trail before morning. Rosa, send in —"

153

But Hatfield interrupted. "Wait, sir," he said, "what you're proposing won't do any good and may do harm. Trying to run down Cartina with a large force in his native mountains is very nearly a hopeless task. We've got to think this out. If we only knew where he will take her."

"*Capitan,* I think I know," Pancho broke in. "I know where Cartina's hidden village is. He will take her there. He has taken other women captives there. I can show the way."

"Okay," rumbled old Tom. "I'll rout out the boys and we'll ride."

But Hatfield vetoed that also. "No good," he said. "You could never make it without being observed. Cartina would be warned in plenty of time to spirit her off someplace else. I even wouldn't put it past him to kill her if he was hard pressed. He's not a man when he's aroused, he's a devil!"

"*Si,*" Pancho agreed. "From *infierno,* to where I trust he will soon return."

"Then what can we do?" old Tom asked helplessly.

"Reckon it's up to Pancho and me," Hatfield replied grimly. "Please have your cook rustle us a bite to eat and provisions for our own saddle pouches, and send word to the wranglers to give our horses an extra helping of oats, water with a little whiskey in it,

154

and a good rubdown. Then with another hour of rest they'll be ready to travel. No use rushing. We've got a long ride ahead of us and we can't hope to do anything, anyhow, before they reach the village with her. Then we'll make a try, and either bring her back with us or stay there with her."

"God grant you are successful," old Tom said, in a broken voice.

"I've a notion we will be," Hatfield said cheerfully. "It'll be the last thing expected, us dropping in on them. And I feel pretty sure Cartina wasn't with the party that captured her. That was handled by that varmint who delivered the fake note. My guess is that Cartina will be notified after she reaches the village. Hope I'm right, for I figure he's the real brains of the outfit and the others should be easier to outwit."

A little over an hour later, Hatfield and Pancho rode away from the Running W ranchhouse. Old Tom remained seated by the fire, staring at the shadows dancing and flickering on the wall. But now they refused to take form. They were grotesque, distorted, bearing the semblance of spectres that leered and gloated. Fragments of a broken dream! A verse of Scripture came, unbidden, to his lips:

"For what hath man of all his labour, and of

the vexation of his heart, wherein he hath laboured under the sun?"

Hitherto Tom Weston had never failed to justify any event which had befallen him. But now — *"Vanity! all is Vanity!"* Was it possible that he, Tom Weston, could have been one of those referred to by the Preacher? He thought of the sister he had loved above all others. Her dryad-like face, with its sweet, elusive smile, seemed to peer at him now wistfully out of the shadows. She had never believed in his mighty dream. She had counselled against it, telling him that it would bring only unhappiness to himself and others. She had gone. And now her daughter was gone.

"Vanity! all is Vanity!"

Weston shuddered, and crouched near the fire as if he were deathly cold.

17.

"So you know where Cartina hangs out," Hatfield remarked as he and Pancho rode swiftly south.

"Yes," Pancho replied. "To go there is madness; his men swarm in the narrow valley."

"Reasonable to believe it," Hatfield admitted. "And you figure we're taking a considerable chance?"

"Assuredly, *Capitan,*" Pancho replied. "You and I ride together to death."

"Perhaps," Hatfield nodded. "But it looked like that before and we came through all right. So perhaps we will again."

"If I can but line sights with that *ladrone,* I care not what happens," Pancho said. "We ride south to the Coronado hills, then turn west and south again by way of a trail little used and known to but few. A trail that seems to have no beginning and no end, and indeed few who ride it ever see its end. For *that* is in Cartina's walled valley."

All the rest of the night they rode and when morning broke they were across the Rio Grande and in the Coronado hills, a jagged and broken spur of the Carmen Mountains of Mexico. Here they made camp for the day, for, as Pancho pointed out, to ride the hidden trail in daylight would be sheer madness. Although burning with impatience and bitterly apprehensive as to Sylvia's welfare, Hatfield was forced to agree with him. Nothing would be gained by barging ahead into what would very likely be disaster. It was not a time for impulsive action, but for cold reason and careful planning.

At dusk, they started anew, following a

trail that wound sluggishly between beetling crags and precipitous hills, boring deeper and deeper into the very heart of the mountains.

Hour after hour they rode, meeting with no adventures or obstacles of a physical kind. Of moral, or rather mental obstacles there were many, since to Hatfield the atmosphere of the place was as that of a haunted house. It may have been the embracing darkness, or the sound of the night wind among the leaves and branches, or the sense of the imminent dangers that awaited them. Or it may have been unknown horrors connected with the place of which some spiritual essence still survived, for without doubt localities preserve such influences which can be felt by the sensitive among living things, especially in favoring conditions of fear and gloom. At any rate, Hatfield admitted to himself later that he never experienced more subtle and yet more penetrating terrors than he did upon that ride between the dark and towering walls of naked stone.

"Is this place guarded?" he finally asked of Pancho.

"Not here," the Mexican replied. "But where the gorge narrows to a gut beyond which lies the village of Cartina, there is a guard whom no one can pass without giving the countersign. There, *Capitan,* our lives will hang upon a single thread. The thread? That none know that I have left the service of *El Gran Generale.*"

"Think he might have recognized you during the row at Marta?"

"It is possible," Pancho conceded; "but soon we shall know. My last word to you, *Capitan,* do not let them take you alive."

Higher and higher towered the mighty walls of stone. And darker and narrower grew the gorge. The click of the horses' irons threw back eerie echoes from the cliff and even their breathing sent stealthy whispers coursing up the encroaching crags. Pancho slowed the pace to a walk. Hatfield loosened his guns in their sheaths.

Without warning a harsh voice challenged from the darkness ahead. Pancho instantly reined in and called an answer in Yaqui that Hatfield did not understand. There was a moment of tingling suspense, then a grunted reply from the unseen guard. Pancho spoke to his horse and they rode on.

"So far all is well," he whispered. "They have not changed the password. Two hundred yards farther on we will see the village."

Soon they had passed beyond the gut. The

gorge widened out into a valley into which moonlight filtered. Hatfield could make out the bulk of cabins ahead. Only an occasional light winked in a window. A deep silence blanketed the sleeping village.

Another hundred yards more and Pancho turned into a dense thicket.

"Here we will leave the horses," he whispered. He gestured to a shadowy irregular rectangle that was set near the left wall of the canyon-valley and some distance from the other and smaller buildings scattered about.

"There dwells Cartina, alone," he whispered.

"Doesn't trust anybody close to him, eh?" Hatfield commented.

"That is right," Pancho answered. "None may come near his house. But look, tonight a guard is stationed by the door. Which means that *El Gran Generale* is not there."

"But that somebody who needs watching is," Hatfield said.

"Yes. It can be none other than *La Senorita*. His men brought her here and now they await Cartina's arrival. *Capitan,* we must not delay; he may come at any moment. But the guard, he must be disposed of, and silently."

Hatfield nodded, studying the terrain. He

saw that there were clumps of brush and a tree or two between where they stood and the cabin door. And the moon cast but a wan glow over the scene. The guard leaned on a rifle beside the door, nodding.

"Looks like he's half-asleep," Hatfield said. "I'll see what I can make of him. No, you stay here. One will have a better chance than two. If things don't go right, you'll have to make a break for it."

"Here I stay till we leave together," Pancho answered grimly, adding, "and *La Senorita* with us."

Hatfield did not argue. He studied the guard for another moment, then glided out of the thicket and an instant later crouched behind the first bush. Watching every slightest motion of his quarry, he risked another advance to the shadow of a tree. He crouched behind the trunk. Now he had less than twenty feet to go, but with only a single scraggly bush between him and the cabin. If he could only reach the wall of the building unobserved, he had a good chance to slip around the corner and be on top of the sleepy watchman before he was able to give the alarm. He took a deep breath and slipped across the open space. He exhaled as he crouched in the shadow of the building. With the greatest care, testing each foot of the ground before trusting his weight upon it, he moved along the log wall until he reached the corner. Now everything depended on the guard either being asleep or looking the other way.

Pancho, crouched in the growth, sandwiching prayers between curses, saw Hatfield's shadow on the corner of the building. The tall shadow hesitated an instant, then glided forward, hands outstretched. The guard turned, but just too late. The Lone Wolf's steely fingers closed on his throat. Instinctively he threw up his hands to clutch at Hatfield's wrists. That was his undoing. As the terrible grip tightened on his throat, he clutched and tore at the Ranger's wrists, then belatedly went for his gun.

Hatfield's left hand flashed back and forward. His fist thudded against the fellow's jaw. He collapsed limply. Hatfield gently eased his unconscious form to the ground, turned and beckoned to Pancho who came sliding across the open space like a fleeting wraith. Together they turned to the door. It was secured by a heavy bar dropped into slots.

"Now if it isn't locked, too, and if she just doesn't scream when we open the door," Hatfield breathed. "Here goes!"

With the greatest care to make no sound, he raised the bar from the slots and passed it to Pancho, who laid it on the ground. Then Hatfield shoved gently on the knobless door. It swung open easily, revealing a dimly lighted interior. There was a choking gasp of fright as he slid through the opening.

"Hush!" he whispered. "It's Hatfield!"

Sylvia was sitting on a blanketed couch on the far side of the room, her eyes big with terror. A swift glance told Hatfield that she was the only occupant of the cabin. With a little whimpering cry, she leaped to her feet and ran to him. He held her close for an instant, her fingers clutching at his shirt front, her breath coming in stifled sobs.

"Quiet!" he told her. "Don't make a sound. Outside, quick!"

They glided through the door together. Pancho was waiting, a cocked gun in his hand. Hatfield glanced at the unconscious guard sprawled beside the wall and decided there was nothing to fear from him.

"Let's go," he told Pancho. "The horses!"

They crossed the open space without detection. Hatfield swung Sylvia behind the cantle.

"Goldy will carry double," he whispered. "Hang onto me tight. We may have to make a dash for it. And hug up close so the guards won't notice Goldy's packing two."

With Pancho leading the way, they rode slowly up the gorge, toward where the narrow, guarded gut was a block of darkness. They reached it and the challenge rang out. Pancho answered as before. The guard grunted a reply. Everything seemed to be moving perfectly.

At that moment a blood-curdling yell seemed to fill earth and heaven, followed by a wild screeching of words Hatfield could not understand. The watchman by the cabin had regained consciousness.

But the guards seemed to understand. Their voices rang out, harsh, peremptory. Hatfield caught one word, *"Alto!"* — Halt!

"Trail, Goldy!" he roared. As the sorrel shot forward he jerked both guns from their sheaths and sprayed the darkness ahead with lead. Pancho was also shooting with both hands and howling like a fiend. Screams and curses sounded and a wild scrambling. Then they were past, the pandemonium behind them.

Guns blazed in the darkness, lead whined past. Hatfield by a miracle of dexterity, twisted about and jerked Sylvia around in front of him, cradling her against his breast as bullets stormed around them. Pancho jerked his rifle from the boot and fired back toward the gut as fast as he could work the ejection lever. Louder yells echoed the reports, and a wailing cry of pain.

"Ride!" Hatfield shouted, "we'll be out of range in a minute."

They were, but the minute seemed eternal with the leaden messengers of death whispering in their ears. One turned Hatfield's hat sideways on his head. Another burned the bay's glossy haunch, bringing forth a squeal of rage. His convulsive forward bound very nearly unseated Pancho. Then they were around a bend and drawing away from the uproar behind.

The going was rough, but they dared not ease the pace. They had to take their chances should the horses fall.

"Now if we just don't meet Cartina and some other hellions headed this way, we'll make it," Hatfield said.

"We make it if we meet *El Diablo* himself," jolted Pancho. "*Capitan,* we are not destined to die yet, otherwise we would have been very dead before now. Never before has one ridden into Pedro Cartina's stronghold and out again against his will. No, we do not die, but others died tonight or I am much mistaken."

"Sounded a bit like it," Hatfield agreed.

165

"Guess I didn't hit that guard hard enough. He came to a lot sooner than I expected."

"*Si,* a knife between his ribs would have been better," Pancho agreed cheerfully.

It was nervous riding through the echoing dark with no way of knowing what was ahead of them; but as they covered mile after mile without incident, their spirits rose. Just the same they were duly thankful when they splashed through the shallow waters of the Rio Grande, under a brightening sky and were safe on Texas soil.

Sylvia's story of what happened was simple. "I had no reason not to trust Calloway. He'd been working for us nearly a month and my uncle seemed to think well of him. So when he told me he had a note from you, I believed him."

"What was in the note?" Hatfield asked.

"It just asked me to meet you at once," she said. "I didn't hesitate an instant. Well, we were some little distance from the ranch-house — I thought we were headed for that thicket where you were holed up — when two men rode out of the brush and seized me. They gagged me, tied my hands and lashed my ankles to the stirrup straps. They didn't hurt me and seemed to be trying to be as gentle as they could. Then they headed south. Calloway didn't come along."

"Maybe rode back to report later that you met me," Hatfield commented. "Well, if he did, old Tom will have skinned him alive and nailed his hide to the barn door by now. What happened next?"

"We kept on riding," Sylvia continued. "Then over toward the trail I heard shooting and I was badly scared, for you, especially as the men with me chuckled most evilly. They never said a word to me, however, just kept on riding. Finally, way after daylight, we reached that village in the valley. They locked me in the cabin. A man brought me something to eat, but would not answer my questions. Nobody would say a word to me. I'll admit I was scared to death."

"You had a right to be," Hatfield said. "Well, it was a damned unpleasant experience for you, but good may come of it. I've a notion your uncle's faith in Anton Page is pretty badly shaken, and he isn't under any illusion concerning Cartina anymore. Now I reckon we'd better find a place to hole up for the day. You're half-asleep, and I don't hanker to go riding north in broad daylight. Had enough excitement for a while."

Pancho was thoroughly familiar with the Border country and soon hit on a faint track that led into the hills. A few miles farther on they found a shallow cave with a spring nearby and a small cleared space in front of it surrounded by thick brush that provided grass for the horses. They kindled a fire in the mouth of the cave and cooked something to eat.

"I like this," Sylvia said as she sat cross-legged by the fire while Hatfield and Pancho smoked. "I always did like camping out. I wouldn't want to be here alone, though. It's wild and desolate."

"Suppose we'd better let you have the cave to yourself," Hatfield suggested, smiling at her.

"Like the devil you will!" she retorted. "You'll stay right here, even if some people wouldn't think it ladylike."

Pancho, whistling gaily, picked up his blanket and walked out of the cave.

"One of us should keep watch," he said over his shoulder. "*I* sleep at the edge of the growth!"

18.

Old Sam Johnson was a badly frightened man. His hands twitched and his eyes rolled nervously as he sat drinking with his two companions, Spence and Hill, in a little *pulqueria* in the River town of Castolon.

"I tell you we got the Devil on our trail," he complained querulously. "The slug that did for Parker missed me by an inch. That big lawman is 'pizen' with a gun."

"What I can't understand," observed Hill, "is why he didn't kill Cartina. He had a first-rate chance to. Cartina was off by himself, a clear shot."

"Sometimes," Johnson remarked significantly, "sometimes there's an *understanding* between folks."

His companions shot him startled glances. "You mean maybe Hatfield didn't want to kill Cartina?" Spence asked slowly.

"Well, he didn't," grunted Johnson, "and as Hill said, he sure had a good chance to. He plugged Parker, Haynes and Tally, and dusted Jasper's coat on both sides for him. Why couldn't he have just as easy have lined sights with Cartina, if he'd wanted to?"

"The other feller, whoever he was, shot at Cartina," Spence observed.

"Uh-huh, and didn't hit him," said Johnson.

The others were silent for a moment. Johnson drummed on the table with a jerky motion of his gnarled hand; his eyes rolled from left to right.

"What I'd like to know," remarked Spence, "is how the heck Hatfield knew we were going to make that try for the Marta bank? How the heck *could* he know?"

"He knew, all right," said Johnson. "Must have gotten the lowdown somewhere. Of course he *could* have gotten it from the inside. Ever hear of the doublecross, gents?"

"You mean Cartina tipped him off?" Spence asked incredulously. "That sure doesn't make sense. Cartina would hardly tip off a chore he was taking part in. Anything might happen, and he doesn't take chances he doesn't have to take."

"No, I don't mean Cartina," Johnson replied, slowly and significantly.

"One of the boys that got cashed in?"

"That's not likely, either. They'd hardly have set themselves up as a target for Hatfield's guns."

Another silence followed. Nobody appeared to want to say what was in the minds of all. It was Spence finally took the plunge.

"You mean maybe — maybe Page —" He did not finish the sentence.

Johnson shrugged his scrawny shoulders. "Well," he remarked sententiously, "it would sort of be to Page's advantage if there were none of us fellers around. We know considerable. And don't forget," he added impressively, "there's just three of us left. Parker, Haynes and Tally done for in Marta. Jasper bled to death on the trail. Just the three of us who know about Page's little scheme. Get what I mean?"

" 'Los muertos no hablan,' " quoted the lean and taciturn Hill.

"Uh-huh, dead men don't talk. We're on a spot. For two pesos I'd start riding and not stop till I get to Arizona or California."

"Liable not to do you much good," grunted Spence. "The railroad's got a long arm. Killing that express messenger was bad business. Oh, I know you didn't shoot him — Parker did that — but we were all in it. If we're caught we stretch rope. Yeah, we're on a spot, all right, with the law, Hatfield, Page and Cartina to look out for."

"I don't think we have to worry about Cartina," said Hill. "Cartina will shoot anybody who's in his way, but he won't pay much mind to what other folks know about him. He's a gone goslin' anyway if the Rangers or old *El Presidente* catch him, and somebody havin' a little more on him don't matter. But with Page it's different. Cartina's plumb bad and admits it, but Page sets up to be a law-abiding citizen. *He* don't want anybody knowing things about him."

"Just what I been trying to tell you," said Johnson. "Somehow Hatfield got wind of what was going to happen in Marta. Some-

171

body must have tipped him off. And if we go out on another chore, how do we know there isn't a trap set? Answer me that one, will you?"

Neither of the others tried to answer. They merely looked uncomfortable. Johnson drummed on the table with nervous fingers.

"Just the three of us, and Page, have the lowdown on things," Hill remarked. "Cartina don't count."

"Well, one thing's sure for certain, us fellers have got to stick together, it's our only chance," said Spence.

"Sure! Sure! we got to stick together," mumbled Johnson. He turned to peer behind him as he spoke. Spence glanced significantly at Hill. The latter nodded, his speculative gaze on Johnson.

What neither noticed was that when he turned, Johnson was looking into the back bar mirror and at their reflections clearly outlined there.

Johnson turned back to his companions. His face was suddenly impassive and much of the nervousness appeared to have left him, as if he had made up his mind to some course of action and was no longer troubled by uncertainties. He lifted his glass with a steady hand and finished his drink.

"Well, I'm going out and find something

to eat," he announced. "They ain't got nothing here but chili and frijoles and such sheep dip. Comin' along?"

The others shook their heads. "We already ate, while we were waiting for you," Spence said. "Go ahead, we'll be here when you get back. Don't take too long, though. We've got a long ride ahead of us. Page is expecting us tonight. We'll talk over what to do on the way."

"Okay," Johnson agreed, and left the room. Hill and Spence waited a few minutes to make sure he was not coming back at once, then hunched across the table and talked in low tones.

"His nerve's busted," said Hill. "If he gets caught, he'll spill his guts to save his own neck. Spence, you and me are on a spot."

"I don't figure to stay there," Spence replied. "Remember what you said a minute ago — *los muertos no hablan!* The quicker we finish him off the better. Be plenty of chances while we're riding over to Page's place."

They grinned at each other, toothily, and with satisfaction.

They might not have been so satisfied with their scheme had they been aware that Johnson was flattened against the wall just outside the open window, within easy hearing distance.

Johnson also grinned, a coyote grin, and slid along the wall to the corner, which he rounded swiftly. Five minutes later he rode out of town. He did not pass the *pulqueria* where his two companions waited.

Spence and Hill waited for more than an hour. Johnson did not reappear.

"Well, I'm beginning to think the old buzzard took his own advice and headed for Arizona," said Hill. "To heck with him! Chances are he won't get caught. We don't need him. And anyhow we couldn't trust him any more. He just saved us the chore by doing away with himself. Come on, let's go. We've got a long ride ahead of us."

They procured their horses and rode east by north.

On a brush-grown bench overlooking the trail, Sam Johnson crouched at the edge of a thicket, a Winchester cradled in the crook of his arm. His lined face was convulsed with passion.

"So! they figure to do in old Sam, eh?" he muttered, glaring up the deserted track that gleamed ruddily in the rays of the setting sun. "Well, the buzzards will find that's a game two can play!"

For long minutes he waited, nervously shifting his weight from one foot to the other, peering and champing. Suddenly he tensed motionless. Far up the trail two horsemen were approaching. Another minute and he recognized Spence and Hill. He drew back the hammer of the Winchester. As the two riders drew abreast of him, talking together, he lifted the rifle, clamped the butt against his shoulder. The black pupil of the muzzle followed the horsemen till they were a little way down the trail, steadied. Fire spurted through the shadows. The muzzle shifted a trifle and again spurted fire and smoke. Two riderless horses dashed down the trail.

Johnson lowered the rifle, stood motionless for a moment, then began picking his way down the slope. He approached the two sprawled forms cautiously, the cocked rifle ready for action. There was no need of care, however. Both conspirators were decidedly dead.

Johnson thoughtfully went through the pockets of his erstwhile companions, removing a considerable sum of money from each. This he stowed away with satisfaction.

"The coyotes will take care of you, gents," he observed cheerfully. He recovered his horse from where he had tied it, mounted and rode east by north.

Darkness had long settled when Johnson

reached Anton Page's ranchhouse. He was admitted to the presence of the ranchowner. Page nodded a greeting.

"Where are Spence and Hill?" he asked.

"Ain't seen 'em all day," lied Johnson. "They eased out on me over in Castolon. Said they'd be back in a little while, but they didn't show. Between you and me, Boss, I've a notion they lit out for Arizona. They talked about doing just that, and they were bad scared over what happened in Marta. Good riddance, I say."

"You're right," Page instantly agreed. "We don't need 'em any more. Sit down and take it easy while I finish this article."

Old Sam sat down, smiling complacently and filling his pipe. Could he have read aright the derisive and menacing gleam in the lowered eyes of the arch-plotter, he would not have felt so complacent about matching wits with Anton Page.

Page took his time about the article. When it was finished, he pushed the papers aside and regarded Johnson.

"Well, what did you learn at Coronado?" he asked.

"That the stage will pack plenty next Wednesday," Johnson replied. "Fifty thousand dollars in gold bars, maybe more. But it's a tough nut to crack, Boss. Guarded inside and out by plumb salty hombres — four in all, not counting the driver."

"Hmmm! Wednesday, that's the fifth," remarked Page. "And what about the cattle that are run to Coronado for sale?"

"Herds coming in practically every day," Johnson answered. "They mostly come from the east and before they hit town they use the west fork of the San Jacinto Trail. That's the trail the stage uses, but it takes the north fork to the railroad. Trail forks about ten miles out of town."

"I see," Page remarked thoughtfully. "Okay, Cartina will be here in a little while. You can pass the information to him. He'll know what to do. No, you don't ride with him this time. He's taking only some of his Yaquis with him. This chore doesn't call for numbers, but smart thinking. Cartina's picking his men carefully. They understand him. He wants to do it that way. You'll be taken care of, but we'll let Cartina run it the way he wants to."

19.

As darkness fell over the wild wasteland, Hatfield and Pancho busied themselves preparing a meal.

"Lucky we put plenty of chuck in our

pouches, seeing as we have a guest," the former observed.

Sylvia, who had been gazing dreamily into the fire, looked up, met Pancho's laughing eyes and blushed rosily.

"*La Senorita* will soon be home, for which, doubtless, she will be thankful," he said with a gravity that his eyes belied.

Sylvia tossed her bright curls. "Oh, I don't know," she replied. "If I didn't know that poor Uncle Tom is worried sick about me, I wouldn't be in a bit of a hurry. I like it here, and I'll never forget this little cave."

Hatfield smiled as he turned the bacon in the skillet.

"I'm not likely to either," he replied.

"I won't *let* you forget it," she teased.

" 'Even the devil retreats from a determined woman,' " Pancho quoted significantly.

"Smart feller," chuckled Hatfield. "Let's eat."

In the dark hour before the dawn, they reached the Running W ranchhouse. Passing the guard at the end of the drive, they rode up to the veranda. A light burned in the big living room. As they mounted the steps the door was flung open and the towering form of old Tom was outlined against the light. He uttered a glad cry and held out his arms.

Sylvia ran to him. He enveloped her in a bear hug and held her close for a moment. Then he gravely shook hands with Hatfield and Pancho.

"Were you terribly worried, dear?" Sylvia asked him.

Old Tom was silent for a moment, then —

"Honey, somehow I wasn't as much as was to be expected," he admitted. "At first, I was scared loco. But when Hatfield said he was going to get you — well, I just figured he would, that's all. After that I was just waiting. I felt sure as hell he would get you away from that mangy scoundrel, and that once you were in his hands there wouldn't be anything more to worry about."

"Huh! that's what *you* think!" Sylvia answered as she trotted up the stairs, smiling at him over her shoulder.

"Now what the devil did she mean by that?" snorted old Tom. "I guess that's why I never got married. I never could understand women, and had sense enough to know it. Now, son, tell me all about everything."

Hatfield told him. Weston listened in silence, nodding his big head from time to time.

"Yes, I guess I was wrong about Cartina,"

179

he said readily when Hatfield had finished. "You were right. He's just an infernal bandit, and if I ever manage to line sights with him, he'll be a dead bandit. But," he added doubtfully, "Page could have made an honest mistake about Calloway."

"Yes, he could have," Hatfield admitted dryly and deftly turned the conversation into other channels. He was content to let the seed of doubt sown in old Tom's mind grow and burgeon.

Weston glanced at the clock. "Guess you boys had better wash up," he advised. "The cook is throwing a snack together. Wouldn't be surprised if you could use it."

Sylvia joined them at the breakfast table, wearing the rather revealing golden-hued robe in which Hatfield first saw her. She colored under the admiration of his gaze; but the dimple showed at the corner of her red mouth.

"Go ahead and *look* all you want to now," she said. "Doesn't make any difference any more."

Old Tom looked bewildered at this bit of byplay, but evidently decided that silence was the safest ground.

"And now," he said after they finished eating, "I'd say it's bedtime for everybody. I didn't have much sleep the last couple of nights and I reckon that goes for the rest of you. And Hatfield, guess you'd better stay out of sight till dark. Not that it matters much in this section. I heard Sheriff Mc-Cauley said the other day that if he met you on the trail, he'd look the other way."

"And Jim, you'd better put some more dye on those scratchy whiskers," Sylvia said. "The roots are beginning to show black."

Pancho chuckled. Old Tom shook his head in mock disapproval and poured himself some more coffee.

"And now what, *Capitan?*" Pancho asked after the good-byes were over and they rode away from the Running W ranchouse in the darkness of a new night.

"Down to the Border," Hatfield decided. "We'll see if we can learn anything. I'm of the opinion that Cartina will bust loose somewhere soon. Missing out on that Marta raid must have tangled his twine for him. He'd doubtless counted on a good haul there. His kind can't afford to sit still. If his men haven't got money in their pockets, they start raising hell and likely as not slide off on something of their own and make trouble. An owlhoot leader has to produce results or he doesn't stay a leader. There is no such thing as loyalty among that kind of people. Cartina can hold his bunch together only so long as he shows more brains and ability. That's been the history of every outlaw bunch. As long as things go smoothly and they're flush, they stick together, but once let the going get rough and they fall apart. Cartina knows that, and so does Page. They realize that they must keep things moving and keep their hellions satisfied. So Cartina will have to figure something else in a hurry. Our chore is to try and find out what that something else is. If we can put another crimp in his plans, he's in for trouble, and once let him get into trouble and the big feller, Page, is also in trouble. He can keep a leash on Cartina just so long as Cartina figures it's to his advantage to stay leashed. Once let Cartina think otherwise and he'll throw Page to the wolves as quickly as he would anybody else."

He paused for a moment, his eyes thoughtful. "And that possibility is our big ace in the hole," he added. "Come the night of the new moon and maybe we'll have our chance to flip that ace over and rake in the pot. But first we want to try and get a line on whatever Cartina has in mind."

"We will go to Castolon, down on the Rio Grande," Pancho said. "I have friends there and in Santa Helena, directly across the River. Men there know much of what goes on in the Border country. Not far off is *Paso de los Chisos* — the Pass of the Chisos — and there the River is shallow and much used by those who smuggle cattle. *Si*, at Castolon we should learn something. There is a trail by which we can enter Castolon from the east, a little used trail nowadays since gold was discovered in the Coronado hills to the west and most traffic now runs from Coronado north to the railroad. But the trail is still there and because travellers seldom frequent it now it is good for our purpose."

"Okay," Hatfield agreed. "We'll go to Castolon."

They rode most of the night and then made camp in the hill country east of where the trail wound around the Rattlesnake Mountains. By mid-morning they were in the saddle again. They passed Tule Mountain, travelling in a southerly direction, then turned sharply west and into a track that showed signs of much use in the past but now stretched lonely and deserted to the horizon.

"Six, perhaps seven miles and we reach Castolon," Pancho said.

They had sighted the thin blue smoke-smudge against the sky that marked the site of the River town when Hatfield suddenly rose in his stirrups, staring ahead.

"Now what the devil is that?" he wondered.

Pancho's *Indio* eyes quickly answered the question —

"Dead men, two of them, lying face downward on the trail."

"Looks like you're right," Hatfield agreed, a few minutes later. "Wonder what hell-raising has been going on here?"

They quickened their horses' pace and soon reached the two sprawled forms, one of a lean, lanky, black-haired man, the other short and squat with bristly red hair. Hatfield dismounted and turned the bodies over.

"Thought so," he muttered. "Curt Spence and Alex Hill. Two of the hellions that made up my troop at Cibola," he explained to Pancho.

"Well," said the Mexican youth, "it would appear that *Senor* Death struck wisely and well."

Hatfield nodded. "But I wonder how come?" he remarked. "Both shot in the back, and with a heavy rifle."

He examined the bullet wounds closely. "Slugs ranged downward in both instances," he mused. "Looks like they were fired from up on the slope." He measured the distance with his eye and focused on the brushgrown bench fifty yards or so up the slope.

"Think I'll go up there and look around," he said. "Might learn something."

Leaving Pancho with the horses, he climbed the slope to the bench. He searched the terrain carefully and soon unearthed evidence that a mounted man had forced his way through the growth no great time before — he had already estimated that the two men had been done for at least forty-eight hours, perhaps a little more. Another ten minutes of meticulously going over the ground and he found two empty brass cartridges.

"That's what did for them, all right," he mused, stowing the shells in his pocket. "The question is who, and why?"

With a final glance around, he rejoined Pancho.

"Looks like this trail isn't travelled much," he remarked. The other shrugged his shoulders.

"That the bodies were not disturbed is no proof that no one passed this way," he said. "An *Indio* would have never touched them, and the same can be said for most Mexicans. Quite a few may have eyed them, and passed by on the other side."

"Perhaps we can learn something in

town," Hatfield suggested. "The spot where the drygulcher holed up indicates that Spence and Hill were travelling away from Castolon. Rather unlikely they would have passed through without stopping some-place."

Pancho nodded agreement.

As an afterthought, Hatfield went through the dead men's pockets but found nothing of significance.

"Not a cent on them, either," he reported. "Looks like whoever did for them cleaned them afterward. That, of course could have been the reason for the killings. They might have flashed considerable dinero in town."

"And somebody rode down here ahead of them and ambushed them," Pancho remarked.

"Could be," Hatfield admitted, "but some-how I don't think so. I've a notion there was some other and more personal reason. Come on, let's get to town and see what we can learn. You do the talking. I believe you said you know some folks there."

"That's right," Pancho nodded. "One who runs a drinking place, among others."

"Bar owners and barkeeps usually know everything," Hatfield commented. "We'll try the saloons first."

As soon as they arrived at the river town,

they tethered their horses at a convenient rack and entered the first drinking place they came to. Over the glasses, Pancho engaged the bartender in conversation.

"We expect to meet a couple of *amigos* here," he said. "A short, heavy-set man with red hair and a tall, lean black-haired man. Have you seen anything of them today?"

The barkeep shook his head. "Don't remember seeing any gents who looked like that here," he disclaimed. "But could have been. Lots of folks coming and going all the time since the mines opened over at Coronado. I'm pretty busy and don't pay much attention."

They finished their drinks and sauntered along to the next place, with negative results. They tried a third. Here the barkeep sort of rec'lected seeing two fellers who looked that way, but couldn't be sure. At a fourth establishment they learned nothing. When they reached the street again, Pancho remarked, "Farther down the street is a place owned by a man I know, a Mexican. Let's pass up the other places and go there. I can talk with him better."

Hatfield agreed and a little later, they entered a small *pulqueria*. The man behind the bar greeted Pancho by name. For several minutes they chatted together in Spanish, of inconsequential matters, then Pancho asked the usual questions. The bar owner replied in Spanish, which Hatfield understood perfectly.

"Yes, *amigo,*" he said. "I recall seeing two such men, two — no, three days ago. They sat at the table by the window and talked. There was a third man with them, a small, gray-haired man with a wrinkled face."

"Sam Johnson, sure as shootin'," Hatfield murmured to himself.

"Any notion where they went?" Pancho asked. The owner shook his head.

"I could not say," he replied. "The small one with the gray hair left first. I seem to recall that he said something about coming back; but he did not return. The others waited for some time, then they too departed. No, I do not know where they were bound, but they came here from Coronado, the town of the mines over close to the New Mexico line. They spoke of the mines there and the cattle ranches roundabout. They seemed interested in both. I listened to their talk because what happens at the mines is of interest to my business. Something was said about a stage and about herds of *ganado* that were driven to the town."

"You don't recall what was said?" Hatfield asked, speaking for the first time.

"Only, *Senor,* that the output of the mines was large and getting larger, which of course interested me. About the stage? Something concerning the trail used by the stage to reach the railroad and also used by the cattle herds to reach the town. Something about the herds delaying or stopping the stage, just what I do not remember."

Hatfield changed the subject and after another drink they left the *pulqueria.*

"Things are sort of tying up," Hatfield remarked when they reached the street. "Looks like there was a falling out of some kind. Johnson must have ridden on ahead, holed up and waited for Spence and Hill to come along. Then he plugged them in the back from up on the bench. Wonder why he did it? Must have had a pretty serious reason. I don't think he would have done it just to get the pesos they may have been packing. Well, anyhow, that bunch of sidewinders is thinning out. Only Johnson, and maybe one other, the one I wounded in Marta, left."

"And soon, *El Dios* willing, those two, if two remain, will join the others in *el infierno,*" Pancho predicted cheerfully.

"I'd like to save at least one till we get him where he's willing to talk to save his own neck," Hatfield remarked. "But this

189

falling out of theirs may give us a first-rate chance to drop a loop on Cartina. If Johnson hadn't done in that pair and left them there on the trail, we wouldn't have gotten the hint that something may be in the making at Coronado or somewhere near. I've a hunch that Cartina and his bunch do plan something there. From what I've heard of the section, there should be some fat pickings for an owlhoot bunch with plenty of savvy. Anyhow, we'll play the hunch. We'll head for Coronado. I've a notion this trail to the west will get us there eventually."

"It joins with the San Jacinto coming up from Mexico about ten miles farther on," said Pancho. "Then we follow the San Jacinto to the forks and turn west again. If all goes well, we should reach Coronado before nightfall."

The sun was indeed only halfway down the western slant of the sky when they reached the forks and turned west.

20.

Swirling white dust tinted mellow gold by sunlight poured from a brassy-blue sky. Drab, unpainted shacks sprawled in the shadow of a beetling cliff. Garish false-fronts shambled along a street that had

190

intended to be straight but had succeeded in resembling a lazy snake making its way across hot sands.

Huge hulks of buildings whose rugged walls quivered and trembled to the endless pounding thunder of the giant pestles of steel did their ponderous dance as they ground the gold-bearing quartz to powder. And everywhere were smoke-belching chimneys, dirty windows, dreary slag heaps, vast mounds of tailings.

The black mouths of tunnels were like blood-clotted wounds at the foot of the mountain. All about could be seen sheds, windlasses, winding gear, pumps, drills, rusty iron and tarnished copper. To one's nostrils rose again and again the fuming reek of sawdust soaked with spilled whiskey; the bitter tang of powder smoke swirling above the sawdust; and the raw smell of newly-spilled blood.

That was Coronado, Texas, down by the Rio Grande!

Coronado! Named for that grand old adventurer who braved mountain and desert, hunger and thirst, savage beasts and still more savage men in his quest for gold, who followed a dream and a vision and rode the trail of legend and fantasy, lured on by the "Cross of Promise" sent back to him by

Stephen, who was black.

Coronado did not find the riches of which he had been told, but — he found a place in which to search for them! And for four centuries the "children of Coronado," fit descendants in name, even though not in blood, of the rugged old Conquistador, were to search for riches in that mighty land of big things called the Southwest; were to search, and find them!

The town of Coronado, built in the lap of a mountain, almost within sight of the silvery "River of the Palms," was a product of that search. Here scarce two years before had been silence and desolation, with only the cry of the coyote and the dismal croak of the condor-vulture to accentuate the silence and render the desolation even more desolate. Here a little band of cowboys taking a short cut from ranch to ranch were startled by the spectacle of a man, gaunt, emaciated, burning with fever, starved, parched with thirst, reeling toward them across the sands.

"Good gosh!" one of the group exclaimed as they quickened their horses' pace. "Good gosh! it's a black man!"

It was a man with a powerful, good-humored face almost black, with a short wooly beard and piercing black eyes. He might well have been a descendant of that Moor called *Estevanico,* that "Stephen who was black" who had been shipwrecked on the coast of Florida and had journeyed across the continent, his destiny to guide Coronado in his search for the fabled Seven Cities of Cibola, whose inhabitants lived in palaces ornamented with sapphires and turquoises, and possessed gold without end.

But this man had found what Black Stephen never found. The frayed pockets of his ragged garments were bursting with gold quartz, and Gabe Jackson had his location notice, his data and specifications all in good order.

"Plenty for everybody, white man," he told the cowboys. "You fellers have saved my life and I'm goin' tell you how to get there."

He did, to the end that those five cowpunchers and Gabe Jackson located and opened the great Coronado mine, so named by Perce Lane, the range boss of the group, who was an educated man and had read and loved the story of Coronado and his search.

An interesting sidelight is the fact that the partnership between the six men was never put in writing. There was no formal agreement. A handshake all around sealed the bargain and although a million dollars worth of gold and more was taken from the

Coronado mine, never were the terms of the agreement violated in letter or spirit.

Other mines followed, and the town of Coronado was a natural sequence. And it was one wild town!

The great Coronado Lode stretched its opulent length through the town from north to south, and on it a half-dozen mines, including the Coronado, biggest and richest, were either in operation or in diligent process of development. These mines, and others situated on newly discovered lodes back in the hills, provided employment for thousands of men who made up the greater part of the population of the town.

It was a splendid population, driving, vigorous, restless. Men! stalwart, muscular, brimful of energy, courage, recklessness. Here was no place for the weakling, the indolent, the cautious. Bright-eyed, quick-moving, strong-handed, the very pick of the world's glorious ones, they poured their superb strength into the mighty effort of ripping the earth's golden treasure from the earth's granite depths.

They worked like Titans and they played like devils. The red blood pulsing through their veins called for hard toil and harder pleasure. They reveled in gold, fights and frolics. They earned big wages and they spent them in a big way. Usually the day after payday they didn't have a cent, but they had pleasant memories.

They lived in little cabins, shacks, tents. They cooked their own beef and beans, sewed on their own buttons, washed their own woolen shirts. They were ripe for anything that promised excitement or diversion. Simple with the simpleness of the strong, easy-going, careless of consequences, they were the material of which "lost causes" are made. The daring exploit appealed to them. The prodigious gamble against tremendous odds for big stakes would catch their fancy, fire their imagination. Small wonder that old Tom Weston had his eye on the men of Coronado, as also did Anton Page.

Here in this turbulent town in the lap of a mountain was opportunity for the ambitious and the ruthless. Here could be the focus of gathering forces that would, unless dissipated or turned into saner and more useful channels, make of the Texas Border country a blood-drenched, fire-blackened turmoil.

The hand of Destiny hovered over Coronado and its shadow was grim and black upon the Border town. But the hardy population of Coronado did not observe it, nor would it have cared if it did.

Cattle ranches surrounded the desert and the hills. Great herds of *ganado* fed on the succulent needle and wheat grasses. The curly mesquite, brimful of the distilled spirit of the vast Texas sun and the sweet rains of the dry country, plumped out the sides of the dogies and made fat steers of scrawny mavericks in a month's grazing. Cattle were so plentiful that markets were always in demand.

Coronado as a ready-to-hand market that did not involve shipping costs was of greater import to the cattlemen than was Coronado's gold. They drove their herds to the mining town, collected high prices and hurried back for more.

But the wealth of the country tempted those who did not like to work for a living. Idlers and cutthroats saw no reason why they should bend their backs over pick and shovel, ride herd in the cold and the wet, or endure the monotony of trade. Not when riches were theirs at the price of a little danger and a little daring. They eyed the herds headed for Coronado, and the gold shipments coming out of Coronado, in pleasant anticipation. Robbery and rustling became quite the fashion in those parts.

Sam Breedman, range boss of the Bar W

ranch, was aware of this fact as he urged his trail herd westward toward Coronado, and it was with a sigh of thanksgiving that he saw, hard and clear against the swarthy uplands, the pale band that was the San Jacinto trail. Straight ahead, he knew, the trail, boring northward from Mexico, forked and the branch that crawled snakily westward was the road to Coronado. Above the beetling crags he could see the dark smudge of smoke that marked the location of the mining town.

"Get going, you work-dodgers," he told his half-dozen cowboys. "Not much more than ten miles to go now. Looks like we've made the trip without trouble. Keep an eye open through that grove west of the creek and then it's safe going the rest of the way. I heard today is payday for the mines. The *pueblo* ought to be sort of salty tonight. The Old Man told me to pay you fellers off when we deliver the herd, and we don't have to head back to the spread till tomorrow afternoon. Understand?"

They did. The prospect of a good time in view, the punchers worked the herd along at a faster pace.

"Careful," Breedman cautioned his men as a narrow winding stream appeared, "that bank is sort of steep. We don't want busted

197

legs on them critters. Spread out, now, and crowd 'em in gentle; they're thirsty and won't make trouble going into the water."

The cows went over the bank without hesitation, sliding and skittering down the steep slope and plunging into the shallow water.

"Why do they keep shying to the north?" little Tommy Whetsall wondered as they closed in on the last stragglers.

"Bank's steep just south of that offset," Hank Turner said. "Looks almost like an overhang from here. Them steers aren't going to tumble over onto their ears. They got savvy."

"They act like something was down there scaring them," grunted Whetsall.

"All right, boys," shouted Breedman, "get them across."

Those were the last words Sam Breedman ever uttered.

One instant, the creek below the offset was a green silence. The next, it was a ragged flicker of pale yellow flame crowned by spiralling wisps of smoke. A hollow crackle of gunfire echoed back and forth between the shelving banks.

Sam Breedman died instantly, shot through the head. Three of his cowboys died with him. The others drew their guns and hurled lead at the pale flickers.

It was a hopelessly one-sided contest from the beginning. Bewildered by the unexpectedness of the attack, appalled by the terrible destruction wrought by that first treacherous volley, the Bar W cowboys made a gallant but futile fight against the drygulchers.

With reckless courage, old Hank Turner sent his horse thundering to the very lip of the creek bank before he fell from his saddle, a half-dozen bullets through him. Little Tommy Whetsall, the last survivor, wounded in two places, shoved his empty gun into its sheath and wheeled his horse in a desperate effort to escape.

A bullet hurled him sideways to the ground and he rolled and bounded down a steep slope into a hollow, where he lay almost hidden by brush and weeds, his bloody head in the shadow of a gnarled clump of sage. He lay limp and silent and apparently dead as dark faces peered over the edge of the bank. His riderless horse plunged down the slope, ran a little ways across the floor of the hollow and halted, peering and snorting.

From beneath the creek bank came seven men, leading the horses they had kept concealed in the deep indenture under the overhang of the bank. Crouching on a ledge beneath the beetling lip, they had been able, unseen, to watch the approach of the Bar W herd and when the riders were within easy range, shoot them down in cold blood. The cattle, scrambling down the bank, had seen them there and had shied away, but the cowboys had ignored the warning.

With a callous glance at the silent, bloody forms, the killers foamed their horses across the stream and up the far bank. They were dark, hawk-faced men, lean and wiry, all except the tall, broad-shouldered leader with a black beard, Pedro Cartina, his reddish whiskers dyed.

"All right," he told his murderous Yacquis, "round up those cows and shove 'em along."

The Yaquis expertly got the herd together and headed it west along the trail toward Coronado.

They pushed the herd along leisurely, intently watching the trail ahead. The scene of death faded away behind them until a straggle of chaparral and a bend in the trail completely hid it from view.

For several miles the trail wound and dipped over the slowly rising ground, each succeeding lip rising higher against the hard blue sky. Finally ahead showed a long rise beyond the dip of which Coronado, less than two miles distant, sprawled in its wide hollow.

Coronado, where there was a ready market for cattle without questions being asked. The raiders, however, appeared to be in no hurry to reach their destination. They let the tired cattle take their own good time. But then, brands are not particularly noticeable after dark even by persons who might happen to be familiar with them and their owners.

From where they followed the cattle, the outlaws could see the crest of the rise. The greater part of the long slope, however, and the stretch of level trail at its foot, were invisible on account of a bristle of chaparral and burr oak.

Not far distant from the edge of the growth, the raiders halted the herd. From where they sat their horses they could still see the crest of the rise. For fully half an hour they lounged carelessly in their saddles and occupied themselves with the easy task of keeping the herd together. Cartina, however, never took his eyes from the crest of rock standing out with knife-edge sharpness against the sky.

As if drawn by invisible strings, a black dot suddenly floated up over the brow of the rise. For an instant it seemed to poise, then it came careening and bouncing down the slope, soon to be hidden by the intervening grove.

The bearded outlaw stiffened in his saddle, called a swift command to his companions. They grouped around him and he took from his capacious saddle bags a bundle of torches made from dry wood. He handed one to each of his followers, reserving one for himself. Flame flickered palely in the slanting sunlight. The torches smoked and smouldered, burning fiercely, giving off a raspy crackling and a strong resinous odor.

Swiftly the owlhoots got the herd under way, pushing it along the narrow track between the growth. Halfway through the grove the men apparently went insane; yelling like fiends, dashing forward until their horses were snorting against whisking tails, flaying the rumps of the maddened steers with the blazing torches.

The stampede was sudden and complete. Bawling their terror, the cattle tore along the trail, prevented from scattering by the flanking growth. The outlaws cast aside their smouldering torches and leaned low in their saddles, black eyes glittering, faces set in hard and cruel lines.

21.

Zack Meadows, driver of the Coronado stage, skillfully tooled his clumsy vehicle down the long slope. Beside him sat a lean, watchful frontiersman, ten-gauge shotgun across his knees, Winchester rifle ready to hand. A second shotgun guard was ensconced in the boot, while two more peered from the windows of the swaying coach.

The stage, transporting a valuable gold shipment from Coronado to the railroad, was practically impervious to attack. Not for a moment did the four guards, fully-armed, relax their vigilance. Zack himself wore a long-barreled six-shooter with which, it was said on good authority, he could shoot the winker from a gnat's eye at twenty paces.

Down the slope rolled the stage, hoofs clicking, springs creaking, rocking comfortably. Zack grasped the multiple reins, with difficulty keeping his six spirited horses from climbing the trees. The guards stiffened to even more alert watchfulness as the dark straggle of the grove drew nearer, although there was small chance of drygulchers hiding among the growth, which would provide dubious shelter and scant opportunity for a successful ambush.

The trail grew misty as it dived into the encroaching tangle of chaparral.

Zack's head suddenly jerked up in an attitude of listening.

"Cattle," he exclaimed a moment later, "coming this way. Listen to them bawl!"

"Coming fast," commented the guard behind him.

From the dusky aisle between the growth burst a terrific vision of clashing horns, rolling eyes and flaring red nostrils. The frantic herd, bawling, blowing, foaming, mad with terror, burst into view like a cowboy's nightmare under a burning bar. Straight along the level stretch of trail they stormed, blind to everything in their path.

"It's a stampede!" cried the guard. "Pull to one side, Zack. Let 'em pass!"

Zack Meadows tried to, but he might as well have tried to pull a grounded lightning rod out of a thunderstorm. Head on the stampede struck the stage. The maddened horses wheeled sideways, cramping the wheels, destroying the balance of the awkward vehicle. Over it went in a wild welter of flaying hoofs, crackling springs and smashing glass.

Driver and guards were hopelessly entangled, stunned, bleeding, fighting for their lives in the midst of the stampede. One guard was dead of a broken neck and Zack was knocked senseless before seven yelling "cowboys" came pounding after the herd. They pulled up beside the overturned stage, shouting in harsh gutterals.

"You loco lunatics!" howled the guard who had sat beside the driver, "let the crazy cows go and help us out of this mess!"

"With pleasure," replied the bearded leader, and shot the guard through the heart.

His companions were blazing away at the same instant. The two remaining guards went down, twitched as a second volley poured into their prostrate bodies, and lay still. The leader flung a shot at old Zack Meadow's body, and turned to help his companions with the jammed stage doors.

They wrenched them free, hauled out the heavy iron strongbox and blasted the lock with rifle fire. Swiftly they transferred the bars of metal and the plump pouches of dust to their saddlebags, mounted and rode down the trail, heedless of the death and destruction behind them and the scattered cattle.

Had they taken the trouble to look back, they might have seen Zack's bloody head rolling from side to side, his lean body twitching. The bullet with which Cartina had thought to kill Meadows had in reality jolted him back to consciousness. Plowing a stinging furrow along his scalp setting the blood to flowing freely, the shock and the pain had wiped the fog from his brain. He groaned, opened his eyes and sat up just in time to see the raiders vanishing into the growth beyond.

Zack Meadows was made of stern stuff. Reeling dizzily, grunting with pain, he got to his feet, wiped the blood from his eyes and stared about with bleared vision. One of the stage horses, jammed against the overturned wreck but still on his four legs, whinneyed plaintively.

Meadows staggered to him, fumbled out his knife and cut the animal free. With a mighty effort he hauled himself onto its back, got its head turned up the trail and beat a tattoo on its ribs with his heels. The horse headed back for town at a good pace.

Meadows twined his shaking fingers in the coarse mane and held on by sheer power of will. Less than half an hour later he was mumbling his story in the sheriff's office.

"They had it all figured out," Zack declared. "Stampeded the herd through the brush and rushed it smack into us at just the right time. They must have been watching somewhere and saw us coming down the slope. Was a slick scheme, all right — just about the only kind to throw the boys off their guard."

"Did you see the brand on the cattle?" asked the sheriff. "Whose were they?"

"Yes, I saw them," replied Meadows. "Couldn't help it; they were scattered all over and I had to ride through them to get here. Bar W was the brand."

"That's the brand of the Worthington outfit over to the northeast of here," said a deputy.

"Fellows who were driving them were Mexicans or Indians, or I'm much mistaken," said Meadows, gritting his teeth as a hastily summoned doctor probed his wound.

"Then we'll find the Bar W riders somewhere along the trail, what's left of 'em," the sheriff predicted grimly. "How did the buzzards put it across on *them,* I wonder. The outfits over east send plenty of men with drives headed for Coronado. They know there's liable to be trouble and are ready for it. Come on, let's get going."

At the head of his hastily gathered posse, Sheriff Crowell thundered out of town. Crowell was a lean-faced, middle-aged man of quiet manner. He was an efficient peace officer and nobody had ever questioned his courage. Some years before he had been one of Captain Bill McDowell's Rangers.

22.

Somewhere in the wild fastnesses of the mysterious purple mountains of Mexico begins the San Jacinto trail. Through canyon and gorge and wooded glade winds its ribbon of gray splotched with sickly yellow and ominous black. Still more ominous are the splotches of red which, unlike the steady colors of the enduring earth, fade from crimson to dull rust as they settle into the dusty soil.

Jim Hatfield was thinking of the San Jacinto's sinister history as he and Pancho rode the western fork in the late afternoon. Ahead, less than ten miles, he figured, was Coronado. Perhaps he would learn something worth while in the mining town that was visited by characters from east, west, north and south.

"Do you think you will be safe there, *Capitan?*" Pancho asked doubtfully. "Someone might penetrate your disguise."

"We'll take a chance," Hatfield replied cheerfully. "Will be pretty close to dark when we get there and most everybody will have started getting drunk. Yes, we'll chance it."

They breasted a low rise and saw, a short distance ahead, a small stream winding between shelving banks. Something caught Hatfield's eye. At the bottom of a little hollow, whose far side slanted steeply downward from the near stream bank, a horse, saddled and bridled, was pawing at some object half-hidden by grass and weeds.

"Looks like somebody might have been thrown," he remarked. "It — say, what the heck's been going on here?"

From behind a clump of brush a second fully equipped horse, split reins trailing, had appeared. Hatfield whistled and the horse threw up its head and uttered a plaintive whinny. As if at a signal, a third animal trotted from behind the brush.

"Come on, let's see about this," Hatfield said, turning Goldy from the trail and heading him down the slope into the hollow.

The object the first horse had been pawing at was moving in the grass. It was a man. He got to its knees and reeled erect, staring about with dazed eyes. His white, blood-smeared face was drawn with pain. One arm hung limp. The other hand clawed uncertainly at a holstered gun.

"Hold it!" Hatfield shouted. "We're not

on the prod for you, feller."

The young cowboy's hand slid from his gun, the wild glare left his eyes, then suddenly returned ten-fold.

"Look out!" he cried hoarsely. "Here they come again!"

Beyond the low lip of the hollow sounded a drumming of fast hoofs, then a splashing in the waters of the creek.

"They'll kill us all!" gasped the cowboy, slumping to the ground again.

"Up to the rim and let's have a look at them," Hatfield told Pancho. He began climbing the slope. The Mexican slid his Winchester from the saddle boot and followed. A moment later they topped the lip of the hollow.

Climbing the bank of the stream were seven horsemen, dark, hawk-faced men led by a tall, broad-shouldered individual with a black beard. He sighted Hatfield and Pancho at the same instant and his voice rang out in command. Hands dropped to guns.

But this time it was Cartina and his Yaquis who were out in the open. Hatfield and Pancho enjoyed the doubtful shelter of the slope. The air fairly exploded to a roar of gunfire.

Shooting with both hands, Hatfield saw a man slump from his saddle like a sack of old clothes. A second screamed hoarsely as a bullet smashed through his throat. A third rider hit the ground with a blue hole between his eyes.

Pedro Cartina, his face the face of a devil, spurred forward and fired down on Hatfield. At the same instant Pancho's Winchester boomed and the gun flew from Cartina's hand, its lock smashed by the heavy rifle slug. The outlaw leader yelled a curse, swung his horse around and sent him charging east along the trail. Hatfield lined sights with him but the hammer of his gun clicked on an empty shell. Before he could shift his left-hand gun into position, Cartina was practically out of six-gun range. Hatfield contented himself with sending his last remaining bullets whining after the Yaquis who were following in Cartina's wake. He saw one lurch in the saddle, the arm of a second drop and swing limply. Then his second gun was empty.

On the rim of the hollow, Pancho was raving like a madman, swearing in two languages and shaking what was left of his Winchester at the disappearing outlaws. A chance slug had smashed the stock at the grip rendering the weapon useless.

"That *ladrone!* Will he always escape me?" stormed Pancho. "Surely his life is charmed!"

"May be for the best," Hatfield replied, reloading his Colts. "If we had done him in, my little plan for grabbing the big he-wolf of the pack would be spoiled. Let him go and let's see if we can find out what this is all about. But first we'll have a look at that cowhand. He's fainted again, from loss of blood, I reckon."

Upon examination, he found a wound high in the cowboy's left shoulder, a furrow in his scalp and a flesh wound over his ribs.

Procuring a roll of bandage from his saddle pouch, he padded the wounds, bound them up and contrived a sling for the wounded arm.

Pancho, meanwhile, had been examining the dead outlaws and the horses that halted when their riders fell.

"Capitan," he called from above, "the saddle pouches are filled with gold, much gold, dust and ingots, and down by the creek dead men in rangeland clothes lie scattered about."

"The buzzards made a raid, all right," Hatfield called back. "Maybe this feller can tell us something when he gets his senses back. Bring some water from the creek in your hat."

Pancho brought the water. Hatfield

washed the blood from the cowboy's face and bathed his eyelids and temples.

"Ought to be coming out of it soon," he decided.

Pancho raised his head. "Horses come, from the west," he said.

Hatfield nodded. He had already heard them. "We'll go up and see if it's another reception committee," he said. "Lots of business on this trail today. Get another rifle from one of those saddle boots."

They climbed to the rim and spotted the new arrivals, a dozen of them, riding swiftly toward the creek. Hatfield drew the makin's from his shirt pocket and began rolling a cigarette with steady fingers.

"Sheriff's posse, I'd say," he observed. "Uh-huh, the old jigger in front is wearing a badge. Take it easy, now, and let me do the talking."

Lounging easily on the crest of the slope, they waited while the posse sent their horses foaming through the creek and up the bank, every man with his hand on his gun and ready for instant action. The sheriff halted them with a gesture and addressed Hatfield.

"What the heck's been going on around here?" he asked harshly.

"Can't tell you overmuch," the Lone Wolf replied. "My partner and I found a wounded man down in the hollow. Then a bunch of gunslingers came from the same direction you did and started a corpse and cartridge session. We managed to down three of them. Four others got away. My partner tells me those saddle pouches are packed with gold. Maybe you know the answer to that."

"I know the answer, all right," the sheriff replied grimly.

Hatfield read suspicion in the peace officer's eyes, and didn't blame him.

"Before you get any notions, sheriff," he observed, "suppose you take a look at my horse and my partner's. They're standing down in the hollow. I guess the bunch you're trailing did some pretty fast riding, didn't they? Those three horses, you'll notice are wet with sweat and their lips are caked with foam. You'll also notice that ours show plainly that they've just been ambling all day."

"Who's the feller you said is down in the hollow?" the sheriff asked as he dismounted.

"Don't know him," Hatfield replied. "A young cowhand. Come and take a look at him."

The sheriff walked forward. Suddenly he seemed to hesitate, a peculiar expression flitting across his face, his cold eyes narrowing a little. Then he resumed his stride. Hatfield and Pancho followed him to the bottom of the hollow, the possemen alert and watchful trailing behind.

"Sheriff," one of the possemen said, "don't you think there might have been a falling out among those sidewinders? That feller's telling a mighty funny yarn, it seems to me."

Before the sheriff could reply, a shaky voice spoke from the grass —

"Fisher, you're a goldarn fool! I didn't think even a deputy-sheriff could be that stupid. These two fellers weren't with that bunch of murdering thieves. They rode from the east and found me and patched me up. No wonder the owlhoots can get by with anything in this section, with the terrapin-brained horned toads we've got for peace officers!"

"Shut up, Whetsall," said the sheriff, instantly recognizing the cowboy. "How you feeling?"

"Pretty good for the shape I'm in, Crowell," answered the puncher. "That big feller did a swell job on me."

The sheriff turned to Hatfield. "How much of a start have the rest of them got on us?" he asked.

" 'Bout an hour now, I'd say," Hatfield replied.

215

"Not much chance to catch them up," muttered the sheriff.

"None at all, I'd say," Hatfield replied. "Pedro Cartina knows every hole in the hills. He and his bunch, what's left of 'em, are in the clear by now. You'd just be wasting your horses to try and run him down."

"Cartina!" exclaimed the sheriff. "You sure it was Cartina?"

"Yes," Hatfield answered quietly.

"Then you're right, there's no use trying to run him down," decided the sheriff. "Look those pouches over, Fisher, and some of you fellers help Whetsall on his horse and lead it up to the trail. And we might as well pack in the bodies of the rest of the Bar W bunch. From the looks of that creek bank, them varmints just about made a clean sweep of them."

As the possemen dispersed to carry out the sheriff's orders, Crowell turned to Hatfield.

"Feller," he said, "it seems to me I've seen you some place before."

Hatfield smiled down at the old peace officer from his great height.

"Wouldn't be surprised," he agreed. "I've been some other places."

The sheriff grinned. "But," he drawled, "you sure must have got a heap older in a

216

heck of a hurry since I last saw you. Guess you boys are headed for Coronado, aren't you? Come along with us. It's a nice lively town, and," he added in lower tones, "I would like to have a chance to talk with you a bit — alone. By the way, I saw Bill Mc-Dowell the other day."

"Hope he's feeling all right," Hatfield smiled.

"He's feeling right good, and got plenty to make him feel good," the sheriff replied. "Tell you about that later. All right, we might as well ride."

Fisher came hurrying to the sheriff when they reached the rim.

"Crowell, danged if I don't believe nearly all the gold those thieves took off the stage is in them pouches," he announced. "These fellers sure picked the right ones to down."

"That's good," said the sheriff. "The mine officers will have something to say to these fellers about it. All set to ride?"

When the posse reached town, the lead horses bearing grisly burdens, the sheriff called a halt in front of his office.

"Fisher, take the bodies down to the coroner's office," he directed. "You can leave that gold with him, too, and notify the mine officials.

"And you'd better go along and tell the

coroner what you know," he added to Pancho. "When you get through, drop in at the
Ace-full on Main Street for a drink and
something to eat. The boys will show you
where it is. Your partner will join you there
later."

Pancho glanced at Hatfield, who nodded.
The somber cavalcade moved on.

Sheriff Crowell led the way into his office.
He lit the lamp, gestured Hatfield to a chair
and sat down behind his desk, regarding the
Lone Wolf quizzically.

"Haven't seen any newspapers lately, have
you?" he asked abruptly. Hatfield shook his
head.

"Well, they're worth seeing," said the
sheriff. "Anton Page is so busy trying to
defend himself against the cashier of the
bank at Marta and the *Laredo Forum* that
he hasn't any time for anything else. The
Forum has an editorial today that raises a
blister, and on the front page is a letter
signed by General Tom Weston in which he
affirms his absolute faith in the integrity of
the Texas Rangers in general and that feller
Jim Hatfield in particular. Seems that Hatfield feller has sure raised heck and shoved
a chunk under a corner."

Hatfield laughed. The sheriff chuckled,
and continued in graver tones.

"Son," he said, "you did a mighty fine chore today, and if there's any way for me to reciprocate, don't hesitate to ask."

Hatfield was silent for a moment, then —

"Sheriff," he said, "there's a little favor you can do me, and do yourself one at the same time. You have a case against Pedro Cartina that will cause him to stretch rope if you can just drop your loop on him. I have it on pretty good authority that Cartina will be at Anton Page's ranchhouse the night of the new moon — that's the ninth, four nights from tonight. Page's place is in your county, over close to the east line. You'd lend a little needed official authority to the chore, so if you can see it that way, meet me in Castolon, the River town, the morning of the ninth. I think we can bag Cartina, and sort of tangle the twine of the big he-wolf of the pack at the same time."

"The sooner Page gets his come-uppance, the better," growled the sheriff. "I'm with you, son, right up to the hilt. How many men shall I bring with me?"

"One deputy should be enough," Hatfield decided. "That will make four of us. A big bunch might attract too much attention, and I figure four can handle it. We'll hit Page's place right after dark. There'll be some Indian chiefs there for a pow-wow, but they don't count. I'd say we won't have to deal with more than four or five at the outside."

"Okay," said the sheriff. "I'll bring Steve Fisher with me. He's always grumbling about something and always seeing things that don't exist, but he's a man to ride the river with."

"Fine," said Hatfield. "Now I think I'll go out and rustle a surrounding of chuck. Been eating sort of sketchy of late."

"The Ace-full I told your partner about is right down the street a little way," said the sheriff. "They serve good meals and the likker ain't bad. And you can get a room upstairs over the bar. Stable right around the corner for your horse."

After Hatfield departed, the sheriff filled his pipe and leaned back in his chair, a satisfied look on his lined face. He was still enjoying his smoke when Fisher, the doubting deputy, came hurrying in.

"Crowell," he said, "you know, that big feller with the gray-streaked whiskers reminds me of somebody."

"That so?" said the sheriff.

"Yes. He reminds me of that Ranger feller, Jim Hatfield."

"That so?" said the sheriff.

"But — but," sputtered Fisher, somewhat

taken aback by the sheriff's noncommittal attitude, "ain't Hatfield wanted?"

"Steve," drawled the sheriff, "if you want him, you go get him!"

"Not me!" Fisher disclaimed instantly and heartily. *"Not me!"*

23.

Hatfield found Pancho waiting when he reached the Ace-full, a big and boisterous saloon already well-crowded. The young Mexican looked much relieved when the tall figure of the Lone Wolf came through the door.

"I was doubtful of that old sheriff," he said. "I thought perhaps he laid the trap."

"You don't have to worry about Sheriff Crowell," Hatfield smiled reply. "He's okay, and he's got plenty of savvy. He spotted me first off, but he never let on. Even when he was talking to me he didn't tip his hand. As a peace officer, it's his business to pick up folks who are wanted. But so long as he didn't 'know' me, he wasn't interested. He took darn good care not to know me."

He then acquainted Pancho with his agreement with the sheriff.

"If *La Senorita* was right about what she told us, and I have no reason to think she wasn't, we'll drop in on Cartina at Page's the night of the ninth," he resumed. "The sheriff has a warrant for him, based on what we told him. Cartina will be in his county and the sheriff is empowered to serve the warrant and put Cartina under arrest. And Page with him, on charges of conspiracy and harboring a fugitive, if nothing else. But I think I can take a chance and be a Ranger again that night. From what the sheriff told me, sentiment is veering in our favor. Getting old General Tom on our side helps to beat hell. Weston is a power in this section, and all over the state. People listen to him. And we sure got a break with that Marta bank robbery attempt. Seems the cashier of the bank is a pretty big man, and he's been raising plenty of dust. All we need to do is bag Cartina and implicate Page and we're sitting pretty. I feel pretty sure afterward I can talk General Tom out of his plan to 'free' Texas. He's already wavering. Finding Page and Cartina using him as a catspaw to pull their own particular chestnuts out of the fire doesn't set overly well with General Tom. He's of a suspicious nature anyhow, I gather, and by now he's sort of looking sideways at a lot of folks. Yes, I really believe I can persuade him to forget the whole business. *La Senorita* is working on him, too, and she packs plenty of influence with him."

"Undoubtedly," Pancho agreed, "which makes the matter a personal issue. *Don Tomaso* would doubtless prefer that a member of his household was not compelled to hide out in thickets."

"Hey there," Hatfield smiled, "you reason ahead of the proved facts."

"The good Fathers of the Mission taught me to speak the English most precisely," Pancho remarked pensively. "Let me see now if I can lay my hand to enough of the barbarous tongue to express what I mean. Ah, I have it! I have conclusively proved, to my own satisfaction, the authenticity of the fact by ocular demonstration."

Hatfield laughed as Pancho spoke, rolling the words on his tongue as if they were sweet morsels.

"You're too much for me," he chuckled. "Well, let's have another drink."

The story of the robbery and its aftermath had gotten around and Hatfield and Pancho were showered with praise and congratulations. They were, in fact, the recipients of rather more attention than the Lone Wolf liked, under the circumstances.

After the weeks of hiding out in the wastelands, Hatfield enjoyed the visit to town. And it was some town! The Ace-full was packed to capacity. Men lined the long bar three deep, every gaming table was occupied, roulette wheels whirred, cards slithered silkily, dice skipped across the green cloth like spotty-eyed devils. Gold earned by bitter toil was thrown away with wild abandon. The sprightly click of French heels and the solid clump of boots echoed from the crowded dance floor. Bottle necks chinked cheerfully on glass rims, voices shook the rafters. A fight started at one end of the bar but was quickly broken up by alert floor-men. The erstwhile battlers wiped away the blood and had a drink together, arm in arm. And in every place along the street the scene in the Ace-full was duplicated. Coronado howled! It was a gay, carefree gathering of boisterous spirits, for the moment, at least.

"Before morning it will be black and deadly, when the red-eye really begins getting in its licks," Hatfield observed to Pancho. "Well, I guess we'd better tie onto a room upstairs and knock off a few hours' sleep. We want to get away from here before daylight comes and folks begin to sober up. No sense in playing our luck too strong."

They rode out of town in the dark hour before the dawn. Only a few late revellers were on the street and nobody paid them any attention. They spent that day and the next hole-up in a comfortable camp not far from the Rio Grande. The morning of the ninth found them in Castolon.

24.

Anton Page paced his office with jerky steps, his face a queer mixture of rage and fear. One moment his eyes blazed with anger, the next they were filmed by a haunted expression. His fingers alternately balled into fists and twitched nervously. His big shoulders hunched forward, his paunch swayed. His legs seemed wooden, unbending, striding with a rigid quality to the joints, like to the twitchy movements of an automaton. He picked up a late copy of the *Laredo Forum* from his desk, glared at it and dashed it to the floor and resumed his nervous pacing. Suddenly he halted and fixed his eyes on Pedro Cartina who sat by the window calmly smoking.

"Well, what have you got to say for yourself?" he spat.

Cartina looked up, his face impassive. He shrugged his shoulders.

"What is there to say?" he asked. "Everything went along nicely till that big Ranger showed up from nowhere and overturned the wagon. Really, it's getting monotonous, the way he materializes from thin air."

The statement seemed to intensify Page's irritation. He swore explosively, waved his clenched fists in the air.

"Do you realize what's happening?" he demanded. "Public opinion is veering away from us. People are asking questions. The Capitol wants to know what the heck's going on over here, anyway. And, among other things, we've lost the support of Tom Weston. And you're primarily to blame for the last. I told you to let that fool girl alone!"

Cartina's face remained impassive, but his eyes glittered like dagger points in the sun.

"Another score to mark up against Hatfield," he remarked. "And that one I won't forget. And while you're pawing sod, remember you were all for the notion when it looked like we would put it over. Would have been a smart move, all right, if it had worked. Your brains worked all right, as they usually do. Calloway did his part. The girl fell for it. Looked like it would be easy as shelling peas. Which, notwithstanding the proverb, in my experience is not simple at all, since generally the shells crack the wrong way and at least one of the peas remains in the pod. So it happened in this case, Jim Hatfield proved to be the pea that would not come out of the pod. And how he outsmarted my Yaquis and slid out of the trap they laid for him is beyond my understanding. But he did, and killed four of them for good measure. Not that I give a damn about that. There are plenty more Yaquis. But just as a matter of mild curiosity, I'd sure like to know how he did it."

"Well, he did it," said Page, "just like he did other things. The whole business has been muddled, that's certain — whoever muddled it." Page looked at his henchman as though he, at least, had no doubts on the point. But Cartina seemed unaware of the implication, and made no reply other than a smile that had a maddening effect on the ranchowner.

"If you think I like the mess we're in any better than you, you're mistaken," he cried. "How in tarnation does Hatfield always know what's going to happen before it happens? What are we going to do to stop him, before it's too late?"

"I gave you my advice once," Cartina returned composedly. "I told you to put a slug through his head when you had the chance. You couldn't see it that way. You, with your brains, had to figure out a complicated scheme that depended on too many factors to be a success."

"The plan was okay," Page defended himself. "It was in the handling of the details that our twine got tangled. If you'll recall, I left those to you."

"And I handled them as they were supposed to be handled, and then Hatfield drops out of a clear sky to spoil everything," Cartina retorted. "If I were in the least inclined to be superstitious, I'd say he is a devil and not a man. Nobody but the devil would be able to figure just what we have in mind and always show up at the opportune moment. And I'd also be inclined to say that some particular devil looks after me, otherwise I'd have been dead a couple of times before now."

Page looked as if he wished the devil in question was not so solicitous about his charge. Cartina smiled thinly.

"I know what you're thinking," he said. "I know you'd throw me to the wolves to save your own hide. Don't try it, Page, it will be the last thing you ever do. If I go, you go with me, don't forget that. You've said more than once that brains win out in the end, but I repeat what I said once before — brains can be spilled!"

Page saw fit to change the subject. "What about the chiefs?" he asked. "Do you believe they are going to string along with us?"

"The chiefs will do what I tell them to do," Cartina replied confidently.

"They'd better. It's our trump card, and likely our last. If we can foment a real rising of the tribes, it will distract attention from us. Will give people other things to think about. And if you can make it look like they are starting a ruckus at the behest of Tom Weston, so much the better."

"Better still if Weston can be made to think that's just what they're doing," said Cartina. "I have a little notion to that effect."

"You'd better steer clear of Weston," Page advised grimly. "Judging from what I hear, he'll shoot you on sight."

"I don't think he'd be particularly averse to lining sights with you, either," Cartina retorted. "After all, it was you who recommended Calloway to him."

"And if Calloway, or somebody, hadn't bungled the affair, things would have worked out beautifully," said Page. "With Hatfield disposed of, Weston would have believed he lured his niece away and would have turned against the Rangers with a vengeance. By the way, where is Calloway?"

"Where people who fail are supposed to be, I guess," Cartina answered. "In hell. The Yaquis didn't feel very good about what happened to them and when Calloway showed up they took care of him, properly. They were glad to find somebody to take it out on. And that brings up another matter — what about Johnson? If you allow him to run around loose much longer he's liable to make trouble for us. He's scared, and a scared man is not to be depended on — something for you to keep in mind, Page. If by any chance Johnson should be grabbed, he'll spill his guts, and he knows too darn much."

"Johnson will be taken care of, after tonight's meeting," Page promised. "That will be easy. There'll be nobody here but him, you and myself, besides the chiefs. I've given the boys the day off and they're all in town raising hell."

"Like honest cowboys should," Cartina observed. "Page, wouldn't it be a nice thing to be honest and not afraid of anybody?"

Page stared. "Well, that's a new line for *you*," he commented. "What started you on that?"

"Oh, I don't know, recent failures, I guess," Cartina said. "I — listen!"

Through the gathering gloom of the late evening came a lonely, eerie but beautiful sound — the call of a hunting wolf.

"Early for *el lobo* to be loosening the latigo

on his jaw," Cartina remarked. "Wonder how that sounds to whatever he's chasing?"

"Shut up, damn you!" stormed Page, the haunted look back in his eyes. "This section just happens to be the wolf's hunting ground, that's all."

"The wolf's hunting ground," Cartina repeated musingly.

Page remembered later, in a strangely inconsequential flash of thought, how Cartina had been struck by the metaphor.

25.

Sheriff Crowley was as good as his word. He arrived in the River town before noon, bringing the pessimistic Steve Fisher with him. But with the promise of action in view, Fisher was cheerful and talkative.

"He never feels right unless there's a prospect of lead flying," the sheriff told Hatfield. "Well, I suppose we'd better have something to eat and then be on our way. Got a long ride ahead of us."

After eating they set out. It was well past dark when they sighted Anton Page's big ranchhouse set in a grove. They pulled to a halt and Hatfield studied the terrain. As he did so, he fumbled with a cunningly concealed secret pocket in his broad leather belt. From it he took the famous silver star on a silver circle, the badge of the Texas Rangers.

"Figure I can risk wearing this again," he said with a smile.

"Didn't I tell you!" exclaimed Fisher. "Now maybe you'll believe me."

"Believed you the first time," said the sheriff, "but you didn't have the courage of your convictions."

"You mean I had too damn much sense to let my convictions get the bit in their teeth," grunted Fisher. "Them convictions ain't changed one bit, either. I figure I'm on the right side of the fence."

The sheriff chuckled, then grew serious.

"Think we can risk sliding in a little closer?" he asked Hatfield. "Don't reckon there'll be a guard posted outside, do you?"

"I'd say not," Hatfield decided. "You'll notice the bunkhouse is dark. Chances are Page sent his hands to town to get them out of the way. I've a notion the less witnesses he has to the meeting the better pleased he'll be."

"I figure he ain't going to be one damn bit pleased in a little while," observed the sheriff as they moved their horses down the slope.

A hundred yards from the ranchhouse,

where the shadows were deep, Hatfield called a halt.

"Got to make sure about things first," he said. "I'd say that lighted window opens into the room where the meeting is being held. The shutters are open. I'm going to see what I can make of them. The rest of you wait here."

"You're taking a chance," warned the sheriff. "If you get spotted it's liable to be curtains for you."

"I'll take the chance," Hatfield returned composedly. "Better than all of us barging ahead into a trap."

He dismounted and faded into the growth beneath the spreading branches of the trees.

"He moves like an *Indio*," breathed Pancho. "I think he will be safe."

Five minutes after leaving his companions, Hatfield was easing along the ranchhouse wall toward the open window. Outside all was silence, but through the opening came the murmur of voices.

Finally he reached a position from which he could peer into the room.

Seated behind a big desk covered with papers, was Anton Page. Pedro Cartina lounged against the wall smoking a cigarette, a look of cynical amusement on his bearded face. That beard, Hatfield noted, had been returned to its ruddy hue, doubtless for the benefit of the half-dozen stolid Indians who squatted in a semi-circle before the desk. In a chair close to the window was Sam Johnson looking nervous and ill-at-ease.

Hatfield noted that an outer door led directly into the room, which was plainly furnished and fitted up as an office. He etched the location of the door on his memory and stole back to the others.

"We'll slide through the growth till we're close to the house," he told his companions. "Then we'll make a quick run across the open space and hit the door. We've got to be all over them in a minute. Cartina is deadly, and Johnson will be a cornered rat. Hard to tell what Page will do. I'm not worried about the Indians. They won't start a fight unless it's forced on them. We have nothing on them, and they know it, and they know the authorities don't favor stirring up the tribes. If things go right, they'll just fade away into the night."

Without further conversation they left their place of concealment and approached the ranchhouse, careful not to make a sound that would betray their presence. They reached the spot Hatfield designated and paused. Hatfield stepped a pace to the front.

"All right," he whispered. "Let's go!"

They covered the open space at a run. Hatfield's shoulder hit the door with all his two hundred pounds of bone and muscle back of it. The door flew open with a crash. The posse streamed into the room, guns out for instant action. The muzzle of Hatfield's Colt lined with Pedro Cartina's broad breast. His voice rang through the room —

"In the name of the state of Texas! I arrest Pedro Cartina and Sam Johnson for murder! Anything you say may be used against you."

Cartina's face did not change expression, but his eyes were terrible. Sam Johnson let out a thin wail of terror and shot his hands above his head. Anton Page seemed stunned at the sudden onslaught. Hatfield half turned his face toward him and spoke in cordial tones.

"Okay, Page," he said. "Much obliged for the tip. I figured you'd get tired of consorting with that hellion, sooner or later. We'll take him off your hands."

Anton Page's jaw dropped. His eyes glazed with amazement, but before he could speak, Cartina's smooth tones cut through the silence —

"Remember what I told you, Page?"

His hand moved like a flash of light. Even as Hatfield's bullet struck him in the chest, he drew his gun and fired point-blank.

Anton Page lurched forward and sprawled across his desk, the whole side of his head blown away by the heavy slug. Blood and brains stained the papers. He was dead before Cartina sagged to the floor. Hatfield shot Sam Johnson through the leg as he dived wildly for the window. The sheriff, Pancho and Fisher trained their guns on the chiefs, who sat stolid and observant, seemingly little affected by the action whirling all about them.

Holstering his gun, Hatfield knelt beside the dying bandit leader. Cartina gazed up at him, the shadow of a smile drifting across his face.

"I told him," he said thickly, "that — brains — can — be — spilled!" With the stony smile still twisting his lips, Cartina died.

Hatfield turned to the chiefs. "Get going," he said, and pointed to the door.

Perhaps not all understood the words, but all understood the gesture. They filed out silently. A moment later unshod hoofs whispered away across the prairie.

"Well, it didn't work out exactly as I planned," Hatfield observed. "I thought when I intimated that Page had tipped us off that Cartina would be here that Cartina would start throwing accusations at him. Instead, he chose to throw lead."

"Simpler and more effective," remarked Steve Fisher, pausing from inspecting the squealing Johnson's bullet-punctured leg. "I 'low everything worked out just fine. And this sidewinder ain't hurt much. Tie a rag around it and he can ride."

"And I think he'll talk, in the hope of maybe saving his own worthless neck, and tie up the loose ends for us," said Hatfield.

Johnson did, volubly, pouring forth information by the yard.

"And I reckon that takes care of things for the Rangers, and for you, too, Hatfield," said the sheriff.

After Johnson had been locked up in the calaboose, Hatfield and Pancho rode to the Running W ranchhouse. Old Tom greeted them warmly and listened with absorbed interest to what they had to tell him.

"And now, General, I think it's time for you to call a halt," Hatfield said. "You see how things can get out of hand. Half a million men died to settle the question of whether this country of ours should be divided or remain in one piece. Don't you think that's enough?"

He leaned forward, earnest, sincere, his

steady eyes fixed on the old statesman's face.

"You know how the great President who was a real friend to all would feel about it," he added. "Your close personal friend, General."

"I will think about it," he replied. "I'll send word for some of the boys to come here tomorrow, and we'll talk again. Hello, Sylvia, here he is, safe and sound, as I told you he would be."

Hatfield and Sylvia walked out onto the veranda, where Pancho was waiting, his big bay saddled and bridled.

"*Capitan,* the time has come to say *hasta luego*," he said. "I ride back to my country. I feel that I have work to do there."

"Till we meet again," Hatfield returned. "*Vaya usted con Dios!*"

"And may He abide with you, *Capitan!*"

With a wave of his hand, Doroteo Aranga, whom the world would one day know as Pancho Villa, rode off to his rendezvous with Destiny and Death!

26.

Hatfield and Sylvia rode to town to take care of a little personal chore, having received old Tom's consent and blessing.

Left alone in his big living room, Weston stumped cheerily about, humming under his breath. The room was warm and cozy, bright with the ruddy glow from the great fireplace. Weston's favorite dog toasted in the heat.

Suddenly the old general paused and glanced toward the wall upon which the shadows of his dreams were wont to pass in review. There was a strange fluttering in his breast, a sudden feeling of thrilling exultation. With wide eyes he stared at the wall, or rather where there should have been a wall. There was no longer a wall!

Instead there was a wonderful flood of brightness, a shining gleaming pathway that stretched high into the starlit sky and poured forth a wonderful radiance.

On that wide, high pathway stood figures, shining figures with radiant faces, Weston exclaimed aloud. There were faces he knew well — faces of men who had ridden with him into Mexico, faces of men who had marched behind him through the bitter mountains of Tennessee.

General Sam, his great captain, was there, chuckling in his beard, and boisterous, loyal Ben McCulloh, and Stonewall Jackson with his steady gaze, and grave Stephen Austin. And standing in the forefront a tall, stooping man with sunken cheeks and the saddest and kindest eyes that ever looked with compassion upon a suffering people. But there was a twinkle in the deep-set eyes and a smile quirked the bearded lips.

Tom Weston started forward, his face joyous.

"Why, Abe!" he exclaimed. "Why, Abe! So you haven't forgotten old Tom!"

Eagerly, happily, he took another step toward the smiling figure, and fell forward upon his face . . .

They buried Tom Weston under the whispering pines on the hill, beside the sister he had loved so well. Many of his followers came to the funeral. After the simple ceremony, they shook hands gravely with Jim Hatfield and departed, leaving their lost leader to sleep with his dreams and his glory.

"I think it is all for the best," Hatfield told Sylvia as they walked slowly back to the ranchhouse together. "Many great men live too long. Sam Houston should have died before the Civil War, at the height of his power and prestige. Instead, he lived to die an impoverished and embittered man.

"And now, honey," he added, "I've got to ride to the Post in the morning and report to Captain Bill. He'll want to hear about everything."

"Ride back to me soon," she said. "Remember, you've got a home now!"

ABOUT THE AUTHOR

Leslie Scott was born in Lewisburg, West Virginia. During the Great War, he joined the French Foreign Legion and spent four years in the trenches. In the 1920s he worked as a mining engineer and bridge builder in the western American states and in China before settling in New York. A barroom discussion in 1934 with Leo Margulies, who was managing editor for Standard Magazines, prompted Scott to try writing fiction. He went on to create two of the most notable series characters in Western pulp magazines. In 1936, Standard Magazines launched, and in *Texas Rangers,* Scott under the house name of **Jackson Cole** created Jim Hatfield, Texas Ranger, a character whose popularity was so great with readers that this magazine featuring his adventures lasted until 1958. When others eventually began contributing Jim Hatfield stories, Scott created another Texas Ranger hero,

Walt Slade, better known as *El Halcon,* the Hawk, whose exploits were regularly featured in *Thrilling Western.* In the 1950s Scott moved quickly into writing book-length adventures about both Jim Hatfield and Walt Slade in long series of original paperback Westerns. At the same time, however, Scott was also doing some of his best work in hardcover Westerns published by Arcadia House; thoughtful, well-constructed stories, with engaging characters and authentic settings and situations. Among the best of these, surely, are *Silver City* (1953), *Longhorn Empire* (1954), *The Trail Builders* (1956), and *Blood on the Rio Grande* (1959). In these hardcover Westerns, many of which have never been reprinted, Scott proved himself highly capable of writing traditional Western stories with characters who have sufficient depth to change in the course of the narrative and with a degree of authenticity and historical accuracy absent from many of his series stories.

We hope you have enjoyed this Large Print book. Other Thorndike, Wheeler, Kennebec, and Chivers Press Large Print books are available at your library or directly from the publishers.

For information about current and upcoming titles, please call or write, without obligation, to:

Publisher
Thorndike Press
295 Kennedy Memorial Drive
Waterville, ME 04901
Tel. (800) 223-1244

or visit our Web site at:

http://gale.cengage.com/thorndike

OR

Chivers Large Print
published by BBC Audiobooks Ltd
St James House, The Square
Lower Bristol Road
Bath BA2 3SB
England
Tel. +44(0) 800 136919
email: bbcaudiobooks@bbc.co.uk
www.bbcaudiobooks.co.uk

All our Large Print titles are designed for easy reading, and all our books are made to last.